HASMONEAN P

518

THE BURKSFIELD BIKE CLUB

Book 1
Mitzvos on Wheels

By Chaim Finkelstein
Author of *Cheery Bim Band* books

The Burksfield Bike Club series
Book 1: Mitzvos on Wheels
© 2006 by Chaim Finkelstein

All rights reserved. No part of this publication may be translated, reproduced, stored in a retrieval system, or transmitted in any form or by any means, electronic, mechanical, photocopying, recording, or otherwise, without permission in writing from the publisher.

ISBN-13: 978-1-932443-46-2
ISBN-10: 1-932443-46-0

Editor: Baila Rosenbaum
Proofreader: Hadassa Goldsmith
Internal illustrations: Jeremy Matthews
Cover design: Randy Jennings

THE JUDAICA PRESS, INC.
123 Ditmas Avenue / Brooklyn, NY 11218
718-972-6200 / 800-972-6201
info@judaicapress.com
www.judaicapress.com

Manufactured in the United States of America

A cloud of dust filled the air as the sleek ten-speed silver racing bike slid to a stop at the foot of the curb.

"Yes!" Avi Drimler pumped his right fist in the air in victory.

He gave his bike a satisfied rub on its well-worn handlebars. It took less than twelve seconds from his house to his friend's stoop. He had broken his old record! Next time he would try for eleven seconds! Thinking about it made him grin.

He ran his hand over his forehead, pushing away a thick lock of red curly hair that never seemed to stay in place. His brown eyes

The Burksfield Bike Club

squinted in the sunlight as he looked up and down the block at the distance he had covered. Victory was sweet! Who would think that Avrohom Yitzchok Drimler, the tallest, skinniest boy in his class, could pump so fast and so hard?

There was no doubt about it. Avi was quick. He thought fast. He talked fast. Everyone knew that there was no one who could beat Avi Drimler from third base to home plate! His quick smile and ready friendship made him a favorite all around the neighborhood.

Avi pulled himself away from pleasant thoughts of speeding, cycling and record-breaking. He had a lot of other things on his mind, like a plan. Everyone in the town of Burksfield knew that when Avi Drimler had a plan you'd better watch out! Once Avi got going, he'd follow through no matter what, no matter how. Avi's eyes twinkled in anticipation as he mounted the steps to his friend Moish's house.

Moish Goldstein and Avi had been best friends for just about forever. Their fathers were both Rebbeim in B.Y.K.—Burksfield Yeshiva Ketana. Their mothers were good friends, too, always sharing babysitting, carpools and an occasional Shabbos recipe. Though Moish and Avi were best friends you would never guess it by looking at them. Moish was short and on the stocky side. He had dark hair and blue eyes

Mitzvos on Wheels

and always looked neat and put together. Moish Goldstein never rushed. A quick joke or smart remark by Moish could keep you laughing long after he was gone, and his smile was as wide and inviting as Avi's.

Avi couldn't wait to speak to Moish. They had made up to meet at six and his watch read exactly six o'clock, right now. As if they had planned it, the door to the house popped open just as he reached the top steps. Out came Moish, his bike helmet in hand.

"Hey, how's it going?" Moish greeted him as he strapped on his helmet neatly.

"Great!" said Avi with a grin.

The boys mounted their bikes and started to ride slowly down the block. Moish rode a blue mountain bike with gold stripes along its sides, which had been handed down to him from his older brother last year. It was a great bike and he took special care to keep it well oiled and in good shape.

"Where should we ride today?" Moish asked. "Do you want to go to Burksfield Park?"

"Yeah," Avi answered thoughtfully. "Maybe we'll find Avromy and Eli."

All of a sudden Moish stopped his bike short. He turned and stared at Avi for a couple of minutes.

"Uh, oh!" he cried.

The Burksfield Bike Club

"What's the matter?" asked Avi, slamming on his own brakes. "Is something wrong?"

"Yes!" Moish cried. "I see *big* trouble."

Avi looked around. The streets of Burksfield were quiet. The sun was shining and the trees were swaying gently in the breeze. Somewhere behind them he heard the buzzing of a lawnmower.

"What trouble?" he asked. "I don't see anything wrong."

"I do," Moish answered. "I see that you have a plan, and that usually means big trouble."

"Hey!" Avi stared at him. "How did you know that I had a plan?"

Moish looked at Avi with a big smile. "Oh, Avi!" he said, waving his hand. "Everybody knows that when your eyes crinkle up like they're doing now it means that you have a plan."

Avi's face turned red. "That's not true!" he said. "You just took a lucky guess."

"Well," Moish went on. "Anyway, that's why I said 'uh oh.' The last time you had a plan we ended up spending four hours hunting frogs in my house."

Avi's face turned even redder.

"Well," he stammered, "I thought it would be a good idea to sell frogs to raise money for tzedakah."

"My mother will never forget *that* plan," Moish responded.

Mitzvos on Wheels

Avi started pedaling again. "Don't worry," he said, "this plan is different."

"No frogs?" asked Moish.

"Of course not!" said Avi. "In fact, for this plan we won't have to bring anything into our houses."

"What's it about?" As usual, Moish was curious.

"Let's wait until we find Avromy and Eli and I'll tell all of you at once." Avi picked up the pace and raced ahead. Moving fast with the warm summer air against his face always made him feel happy and alive. Thoughts of frogs and other minor mistakes took a back seat in his mind as he rounded the curve and saw the big stone gates of Burksfield Park. From the corner of his eye he saw Moish right behind him and together they zoomed down the big hill to the entrance of the park. They slowed down as they passed the pretty fountain right beyond the park's gates. There were always a lot of little kids and strollers in this area of the park and they had to be careful.

They followed the bike trail towards the ball fields. Sure enough, there were Avromy and Eli, as usual tossing that ball back and forth between them. It was rare to see the two boys without some kind of ball sailing between them. If it wasn't a football, it was a basketball; and if it wasn't a basketball it could be just about anything else!

The Burksfield Bike Club

Both Avromy and Eli were brown-haired, brown-eyed and athletic. They were fun and interesting and liked a lot of the same things, such as pistachio ice cream, and both were really good in math. Whenever there was a joke or story to share, it was Avromy whose voice you'd hear and whose hands you would see flying around overhead. Avromy had a big voice with a hearty laugh—you could always tell where Avromy was sitting in the lunchroom without looking around much. And chances were, when you located him you'd want to go sit next to him.

When Eli moved into Burksfield three years ago he was shy and quiet. Avromy was the first to welcome him and help him make friends in the class. Though he was always a serious and studious boy, Eli soon fit right in and made many friends. His talents on the ball field didn't hurt either, and he was always one of the first picked for a team. Avromy and Eli stayed close friends and seemed to enjoy both their similarities and their differences.

"Hey!" Moish shouted, waving to get their attention. The four friends greeted each other happily and all began to talk at once. They had left each other only a few hours ago at day camp, but there was still a lot to report.

"Uh oh," said Avromy. "I see that Avi has a plan again."

Mitzvos on Wheels

Avi looked shocked.

"How can everyone read my mind?" he cried. "Is my head made of glass?"

"It's very easy," Avromy answered. "You always get that look in your eyes when you have a plan. Your eyes crinkle up and your eyebrows point down."

"What is it this time?" Eli asked. "I had a lot of fun with the frogs last time. It's too bad we didn't get a chance to put those tiny pairs of tzitzis on them. They really *looked* like Jewish frogs. I'm sure lots of people would have bought *Jewish* frogs at the Burksfield *Jewish* Festival."

Moish shuddered as he remembered that terrible mess, but Avi hardly paused.

"No, no, no!" Avi cried. "No frogs! This time I think we need to do something more serious."

"And less slimy," added Eli.

"What did you have in mind?" asked Moish.

"Well," said Avi, "I was thinking that maybe we should go into business."

"What kind of business?" asked Avromy. As the son of Burksfield's biggest businessman, Lester Froob, Avromy was very interested in this subject. His father sometimes let Avromy work in his appliance store, "FROOB'S FANTASTIC FRIDGES. Everyone knew that Avromy, like his father, could sell anything to anyone.

Avi stroked his chin thoughtfully. "I was

9

The Burksfield Bike Club

thinking," he said, "that we should start a club so we could have some fun."

"What kind of fun?" asked Eli.

"Well," answered Avi, "we all love riding our bikes. Maybe we could do something that has to do with bike riding."

"Like making deliveries?" asked Avromy.

"Maybe," Avi replied.

"I don't know," answered Avromy. "Most stores already have delivery boys working for them."

"I know!" said Eli. "We live in Burksfield and we'll be riding our bikes. Let's call ourselves the 'Burksfield Bike Club.'"

Eli went over to his bike, which was resting against the nearest tree. As usual his kickstand had come loose. Eli's bike was always in need of some kind of repair. Usually he fiddled with it himself—taping or tying together all kinds of parts that made his bike one of a kind. Now he reached into a small leather bag that he had attached to the back of the seat. He took out a pen and notepad and handed them over to Avi with a flourish.

Avi began to write furiously. "I love it!" he cried. "How does this sound, guys?" Avi loudly cleared his throat and read from his pad in his most important sounding voice.

"*The Burksfield Bike Club.* Always on the move! Call us anytime, anywhere."

The boys cheered and showed their approval

Mitzvos on Wheels

with some fake punches and slaps on the back.

"We'll be famous!" Avi looked off into space, dreaming and planning.

"That's excellent!" cried Avromy. "We can print up signs and business cards."

"Um ... guys?" said Moish, scratching his head. "I have a little problem with this ..."

"What's the problem?" Avi's mind came back from its wanderings.

"Well," said Moish, "it's very nice to have a club with a nice name, but ..."

"But what?" asked Avromy.

"But ..." Moish said slowly and deliberately, "... what in the world does our club do? Our sign says that people should call us. *Why* should anyone call us if we don't do anything?"

"Hmm," said Avi, "you have a good point."

Avi wasn't really disturbed by this minor point but he did pause. The other boys nodded their heads in agreement. Avi blushed and Avromy gave one of his big, good-hearted laughs.

"I guess we got a little carried away!"

Avi looked down at his watch. "Uh oh!" he said. "Mincha is starting in five minutes. We'd better ride over to shul. We'll have to talk more later."

The boys quickly pedaled the three blocks to Anshei Burksfield. At one time, it had been one of the biggest shuls in town. Over the years,

The Burksfield Bike Club

as the neighborhood expanded, other newer shuls had opened. They were closer to where most people lived and shopped. Today, Anshei Burksfield was the smallest minyan in town. This didn't matter to the people who davened there; they knew that their shul was the warmest and the friendliest. The people who davened at Anshei Burksfield came from many different backgrounds, but all were kind and respectful of one another.

There was Rabbi Goldenberg, the aged rabbi of the shul. His father had been the Rav before him and he considered it his life's mission to keep the shul going. Old Reb Yankel Silver was the *gabbai* of the shul. He was well into his nineties and a bit hard of hearing, yet he never missed a minyan. Behind him sat Tzvi Abayakov, who had come from Russia just a few years earlier. He was a tall, strong man with a warm *neshama*. Tzvi owned the only hardware store in town, but no matter how busy his store got he was always involved in one *chessed* project or another.

When the boys walked into shul they immediately sensed that something was wrong. Everyone was quiet. Even Ruby and Milton Greenberg were quiet. These two eighty-year-old brothers always sat in the back of the shul making jokes, but today they looked worried. Rabbi Goldenberg was in the front of the shul talking to Tzvi.

Mitzvos on Wheels

The Burksfield Bike Club

Rabbi Goldenberg looked even more bent over than usual, and had the saddest look on his face.

Avi hurried over to his father who was there to daven.

"Hi, Ta, What's the matter?" he whispered to his father. "Why does everyone look so sad? It's like Tisha B'Av in here."

"Shh, Avi," said Rabbi Drimler, putting his finger to his lips. "They're about to start Mincha."

It wasn't easy for Avi to concentrate on his davening. His *yetzer hara* wanted him to think more about his club idea and the sad atmosphere in shul than about his tefillos; but he did the best he could.

Avi had planned to speak to his father right after davening but before he could begin he found old Mr. Seltzer standing in front of him.

"Oy, Avi," he said in his thick accent. "You answer Amein so vunderfully. It makes mein heart jump to hear you. I broughts you some chocolates today. You vant some?"

Since Avi was a small boy old Mr. Seltzer always brought prizes to shul. Any boy who answered Amein would get a treat from this kind man's pockets. Sometimes it was chocolate, sometimes gum. One time it had even been a pickle, but a treat it always was.

"Thank you, Mr. Seltzer," said Avi, taking the chocolate.

Mitzvos on Wheels

"Vair's mein bracha?" asked Mr. Seltzer with a smile on his face.

Avi made a shehakol very loudly, and Mr. Seltzer made a very loud Amein.

"Dus is nachas," he said with a big grin. "Denk you, Avi, your bracha made mein day."

Avi turned around to find that his father had already begun learning with his chavrusa in the back of the shul.

Avi turned to Tzvi. "Tzvi," he began worriedly, "what's going on? Why is everyone so sad? Is somebody sick?"

"No, no, Avi," Tzvi answered. "Nobody is sick. We're all just a little disappointed."

"Why are you disappointed?"

"Well," Tzvi sighed, "you see, Rabbi Goldenberg had been very excited about starting a yeshiva in memory of his father. There are many new families in our community that have just arrived from Iran, and Rabbi Goldenberg wanted to set up a yeshiva for their children in the basement of this shul, with classrooms and a small Bais Medrash."

"Wow!" said Avi. "What a great idea."

"Yes," said Tzvi, "only it takes money to open a yeshiva. We've just found out that Rabbi Goldenberg will need about twenty thousand dollars to get the school open. That's a lot of money to raise before September."

The Burksfield Bike Club

"Oh," said Avi glumly. "Now I understand why everyone looks so sad."

"Yes," said Tzvi. "Everyone in the shul has been very excited about the idea."

Tzvi looked down at his watch. "I'm sorry, Avi, " he said as he headed for the door. "I have to get home now."

"Goodbye, Tzvi," Avi said with a wave of his hand.

Avi's hand did not rest for a minute. It went straight from waving at Tzvi to stroking his own chin.

"Hmm," he said thoughtfully as a smile grew on his face. His eyes crinkled up in just that special way and his eyebrows turned down.

"Oh no!" came a shout from behind him. "He's doing it again."

Avi turned around to see Moish and the other boys staring at him.

"What am I doing?" asked Avi.

"You're hatching another plan," said Moish.

"More frogs?" asked Eli hopefully.

"No," said Avi. "I have a great idea for our club."

"What is it?" asked Avromy. He was ready!

The boys left the shul and headed toward their bikes. As they mounted and strapped on bike helmets Avi told them everything that Tzvi had told him.

16

Mitzvos on Wheels

"Oh," said Avromy, "that's why everyone looked so sad. I was wondering."

"Yeah," agreed Eli. "I was getting a little worried myself."

"But what does a yeshiva for Iranian boys have to do with our Burksfield Bike Club?" asked Moish.

Avi smiled. "We are going to use our bikes to raise the money for that yeshiva," he announced proudly.

"How are we going to do that?" asked Avromy.

"It's very simple," said Avi, his eyes bright and confident.

"It is?"

"How?"

Avi stopped his bike and pointed to an overflowing garbage can on the corner. "That's how!" he answered proudly.

"We're going to sell garbage?" asked Eli.

"I guess it's better than frogs," said Moish doubtfully.

"No, No!" cried Avi. He practically fell of his bike. "What do you see on top of that garbage can?"

"Well," said Avromy, "I see a banana peel, a candy bar wrapper, and an empty soda can."

"Aha!" shouted Avi. "That's it!"

"Um ... Avi," said Moish, scratching his head. "Are you sure you're feeling well?"

"I'm feeling great!" Avi answered.

The Burksfield Bike Club

"Then why are you so excited about garbage?" asked Moish slowly and patiently.

"The can!" Avi pointed frantically. "The can!"

The boys looked at each other in confusion.

"Well," said Eli slowly, "that garbage can *is* painted a pretty green color."

"No," laughed Avi, "not the garbage can. I'm pointing to the soda can on top of it. Somebody threw the soda can away."

"Of course they did!" said Moish. "The soda can didn't climb into the garbage by itself!"

"Exactly!" said Avi. "The can didn't get there by itself. Somebody threw it out, even though they could have brought it back to the store and gotten a nickel for it."

"Ahh," said Avromy. "I think I'm catching on to Avi's idea."

"Well I'm not," said Moish. "Could you please explain it to me?"

"I think that Avi is planning on us collecting empty cans to raise money for the new yeshiva."

"That's exactly right," said Avi with a grin. "Many people are too lazy to return their empty cans and just throw them away. Lots of people would be happy to give them to tzedakah."

All the boys smiled and nodded their heads.

"You know what, Avi," said Moish, "even I have to admit that this plan sounds pretty good."

"I think," said Avromy, "that we should

Mitzvos on Wheels

change the name of our club. Let's call it 'The Burksfield Bike Club—Mitzvos on Wheels.'"

"That sounds great!" said Avi. "Let's meet at my house tomorrow and we'll get to work."

• • •

The next day was a hard one for Avi. He could hardly focus during learning groups at day camp. Even a baseball game couldn't take his mind off the new project. His mind swirled with ideas and schemes to make this new "Mitzvah Club" work.

Finally, the time came for the boys to meet. They gathered in Avi's garage, now their un-official clubhouse. Amid storage boxes, old bikes, the lawnmower and other assorted clutter, the boys had carved out for themselves a square, clean corner of the garage. Here was where they conducted all their important and official business. Many an interesting conversation and all kinds of imaginative games had bounced around these walls. It was a special place for the four boys. Like Avi, the other boys had been thinking of the new project all day. Now they put their heads together and shared their ideas.

"I was wondering," brought up Moish worriedly, "just how we are going to collect these cans. Will we be digging through garbage cans all over town?"

The Burksfield Bike Club

"No way," said Avi, waving his hand. "We don't have to do that. We can go door to door and just collect empty cans from people's houses."

"That's a great idea," said Avromy. "Let's print up flyers and put them under people's doors. We'll ask them to save their cans for us to pick up."

Avi grabbed a pen and began to write. He read out loud as he went along:

> Please Donate Any Bottle Or
> Can That You Can!
> Save your empty bottles and cans.
> On Sunday, the Burksfield Bike Club—
> Mitzvos on Wheels will pick them up,
> and the deposit money will be
> given to tzedakah.

"That sounds great!" said Eli.

Avromy spoke up. "I'll make copies of this on the copy machine in my father's store. He lets me use it whenever I want to. When it's done we can talk about how we're going to get it all over town."

The boys were very pleased with their plan. Things seemed to be moving along quickly and efficiently. After having done what they considered a respectable amount of important planning, the boys moved from the garage to Avi's kitchen. Refreshments were definitely in order

Mitzvos on Wheels

and the boys took advantage of the Drimler's well-stocked freezer. After working their way through an impressive number of freeze pops, some cookies and as much lemonade as they could find, they ran out to their bikes and headed to Anshei Burksfield for Mincha.

They arrived right on time and moved into their regular places. Eli and Avromy went off to the right side of the shul while Moish and Avi sat in the area where their fathers davened on Shabbos. Mincha at the shul was carried out in the usual calm and familiar way. After davening, all four boys joined Tzvi Abayakov and told him about their new plan to help Rabbi Goldenberg and his yeshiva.

Tzvi grinned from ear to ear. "I'm very proud of you boys for wanting to do such a big Mitzvah. It's a big challenge to raise such a large amount of money. Every little bit will help – even your dimes and nickels. Please let me know if I can help you in any way."

He shook hands warmly with each of the four boys and wished them well.

Tzvi's encouraging words made Avi, Moish, Avromy and Eli feel confident and important. They could hardly wait till the flyers would be ready and for the real work to begin.

The next morning, each member of the Burksfield Bike Club woke up to an exciting surprise. A big square box appeared on each of their doorsteps. "What is that?" squealed Avi's four-year-old brother Shmulie. "Is it your birthday, Avi? Did somebody get you a birthday present?"

Avi couldn't imagine what the bulky package was, but it had his name written on it in big black letters. He quickly tore open the wrapping paper.

"It's a bicycle basket!" he shouted. "It's from Tzvi Abayakov's store!"

Little Shmulie scratched his head. "You're going on a picnic?" he asked his big brother.

Mitzvos on Wheels

"No, silly!" Avi answered with a grin. "Tzvi must have wanted to make it easier for us to collect cans, so he gave me a basket for my bike."

That afternoon the members of the Burksfield Bike Club met in front of Moish Goldstein's house. They were all happy and excited, and proudly displayed their shiny new baskets hooked onto their handlebars. Avromy distributed a stack of flyers, and each boy picked a section of town and decided what streets they'd be working on. They couldn't wait to let everyone know that they were in business.

Avi had chosen the east side of town. He peddled furiously to his first stop on Elk Road. "Wait a minute," he thought to himself. "I can't ride my bike across people's lawns, and I can't throw flyers from the sidewalk to people's front steps either. I'm going to have to get off my bike and walk to each door."

Avi leaned his bike against a tree, took a stack of flyers from his bicycle basket, and walked toward the first house on the block. He went up the front steps, bent down and neatly placed a flyer in the center of the welcome mat in front of the door.

"That was easy," he thought to himself. "Only forty-nine houses to go. How long can that take?" Then, Avi heard a noise that made him freeze in

The Burksfield Bike Club

his tracks. A deep growling sound was coming from the bushes in front of him.

"Uh oh," he said to himself. "Someone or something is not happy that I'm here right now."

Suddenly, from behind the bushes a huge black dog jumped out and landed right in front of him. It began to bark loudly, and furiously. Avi got so scared that he threw all the papers up in the air. The big dog looked at the papers flying all around him and began to bark even louder. It didn't seem to appreciate Avi messing up his yard.

Avi was so scared he couldn't breathe. His mind raced furiously. He definitely remembered learning that there was a pasuk that a person should say if a dog attacked him. He knew that it was from the parsha of Yetzias Mitzrayim, but right now the only thing he could remember about Yetzias Mitzrayim was the Mah Nishtana. Suddenly, the door to the house flew open and a tall, black-haired lady came out.

"Blacky!" she said sternly. "Stop barking! Leave the boy alone!" The dog looked up at the tall lady, gave one last bark and quickly ran away.

Avi began to breathe again. "Th-thank you," he stammered gratefully.

"I'm sorry," she said. "Blacky is just a puppy and she likes to play."

"That was playing?" thought Avi, trying to

Mitzvos on Wheels

The Burksfield Bike Club

catch his breath. "If that was playing, then I really wouldn't want to see that dog when it gets angry!"

"Here, let me help you pick up your papers." In a short time all the flyers were back in a neat pile in Avi's hand.

"What does this say?" She scanned the flyer. "You're collecting cans for tzedakah? Who is tzedakah? Why does he need cans?"

"No, no," said Avi quickly. "That says tzedakah. It's the Hebrew word for charity. We're collecting cans to raise money for charity."

"Oh," said the lady. "I'm Jewish. I should have known that. My name is Mrs. Berkowitz and I'd love to help you out. I'll give you some cans. Wait right here. I'll only be a minute."

As Mrs. Berkowitz walked back into her house, Avi's eyes darted nervously around the yard looking carefully for Blacky. Soon the door opened again. "Here, take this bag of cans for charity. That's a big matzah, right?"

"You mean a mitzvah," answered Avi, as politely as he could.

"Right!" Mrs. Berkowitz laughed good-naturedly. "I should have known that, too! Well, come back again soon. I'll save all my cans for you."

"Great!" Avi smiled. "Giving tzedakah really is a big Mitzvah. Thank you very much for the cans. Goodbye."

Avi looked at the large bag of cans in his hand

Mitzvos on Wheels

and quickly forgot all about the scary meeting he had just had. "Wow!" he said to himself, "our first bunch of cans. There must be at least twenty in this bag." He couldn't wait to show the other boys. He quickly put the bag into his new bicycle basket and started walking over to the next house. After thinking a little bit, he pulled out a pen and scrap of paper from his pocket and wrote down the name and address of Blacky and his owner.

Avi's father sometimes gave classes for *Yidden* who didn't know much about *Yiddishkeit*. Maybe this lady would want an invitation. Avi stuffed the paper into his pocket, and with a happy heart he continued from house to house putting flyers on doorsteps. Of course, for the rest of the afternoon, he kept a sharp eye out for any "playful" dogs!

In another two hours, the job was done. Avi's back ached from all the bending, but he was very excited to have finished the job. He hopped back onto his bike and rode quickly towards Anshei Burksfield. It was almost time for Mincha, and he couldn't wait to see how his friends had made out.

After parking his bike in front of the old building, he quickly grabbed the bag from his bike basket and ran inside the shul. The big bag of cans rattled and banged as he scrambled through the entryway and past the coat racks.

The Burksfield Bike Club

Some hangers got caught on the bag and came down in a tangle. As soon as he appeared in the doorway of the shul twenty-two pairs of eyes turned to stare at the source of all the noise. Avi's face turned red as he quickly tried to silence the noisy bundle in his hand. The men went back to their learning and conversations. Moish, Avromy, and Eli quickly surrounded Avi as they hustled back out into the hallway.

"You got cans already?" Eli cried in an excited voice.

"Did you have to walk and bend as much as I did?" asked an exhausted Avromy. Poor Avromy's face was still bright red and dripping with sweat. "I've never gotten so much exercise in my life," Avromy moaned.

"*Shhh!*" said Avi, his finger to his lips. "They're about to start Mincha. Let's go in. We'll talk later."

At first, Avi thought that he wouldn't be able to concentrate on his tefillah. But then he realized he had a lot to daven for. He wanted his plan to succeed; he wanted the yeshiva to be able to open in September. The only way his plan could succeed was if he asked Hashem for help. He applied himself to the davening, trying to say each word slowly and carefully.

As soon as davening was over, Mr. Seltzer was standing beside Avi.

"Vat vas dat recket you vas making with that

Mitzvos on Wheels

beg of kens? Vy you got a beg mit kens? You vas thoisty and drank dem all up?"

"No, Mr. Seltzer," answered Avi. "My friends and I are collecting cans to raise money for Rabbi Goldenberg's new yeshiva."

A huge grin broke out across Mr. Seltzer's face. "Dat's beautiful! Vonderful! Such nice boyehs!" Mr. Seltzer turned to Reb Yankel the *gabbai*, who was busy putting away the pushkas.

"Nu, Reb Yankel," he called out with pride. "Did you hear vat the boyehs are doing? They're collecting tin kens for the yeshiva."

Reb Yankel looked up in amazement. "They're collecting pens for the meshiga? Why do meshiga people need pens?"

"No, no, Reb Yankel," Mr. Seltzer yelled into the old man's ear. "The boyehs are collecting soda kens to raise money for the yeshiva."

"Oh, for the yeshiva. That's very nice. Here," he reached into his pocket. "I'll donate a pen."

Mr. Seltzer just smiled, patted Avi on the head and walked away. Reb Yankel shrugged his shoulders, put the pen back into his pocket and went back to the pushkas. The boys all gathered around once again to compare their experiences.

"Nu, Eli and Moish?" asked Avromy excitedly. "Did you give out all your flyers?"

The Burksfield Bike Club

"Yeah, we did," Moish said. "But where did you get the cans from, Avi? I thought we weren't supposed to start collecting them yet."

Avi quickly told about the adventures of his day. Then each boy had his own story to share. Eli had given out his papers while on roller skates. Unfortunately, he had forgotten about the extremely steep hill on Oak Road. He flew down the hill faster than a rocket, with all of his flyers flying through the air behind him. It had taken him an extra twenty minutes to climb back up the hill collecting his flyers with one hand and carrying his skates in the other.

Moish and Avromy had apparently had a much easier time. They gave out all their flyers and met a few people who, like Mrs. Berkowitz, were eager to donate their cans.

• • •

The next few days could not pass quickly enough for the boys. They couldn't wait for Sunday to come. How many cans would they get? How much money could they raise for the yeshiva? These questions filled their minds all the time. Every second the boys spent together they talked about their mitzvah project.

Erev Shabbos arrived and Avi was trying very hard to focus on his shoes while he polished them.

Mitzvos on Wheels

Unfortunately, as he imagined himself holding a gigantic bag of cans, he was actually polishing his left hand. Up and down, in nice even strokes, his fingers grew blacker and blacker.

Just then, his little brother Shmulie came into the room.

"Avi, did you hear?"

"Hear what?" asked Avi, coming out of his daydream.

Shmulie noticed what Avi had been doing. "Hey, Avi, why are you polishing your hand?"

Avi's face turned red as he looked down at his very black hand.

"Er, I did it *lekavod* Shabbos, of course," he answered quickly.

Shmulie's eyes opened wide in amazement. "You did?" he asked.

Avi quickly changed the subject. "Anyway, what did you come to tell me, Shmulie?"

"Oh, yeah," answered Shmulie, suddenly remembering his exciting news. "Mommy just told me that we're having company for Shabbos."

Avi's face lit up. "Who's coming?" he asked excitedly.

"You have to guess!" Shmulie put on a sly grin.

"Oh, come on, Shmulie," Avi tried not to get annoyed at his younger brother. "Just tell me who?"

"I'll give you a clue," said Shmulie in a teasing voice. "Her name starts with an S."

The Burksfield Bike Club

"*Her* name?" asked Avi. "And it starts with an S? Who could that be?"

Little Shmulie couldn't hold the news in any longer. "It's Tanta Hadassah!" He gave a little dance around the room and knocked over the shoe polish.

"Tanta Hadassah?" Avi picked up the shoe polish and looked sadly at his blackened hand. "Her name doesn't start with an S."

"Oh, yes it does," answered Shmulie with a grin. "You know her other name, don't you?"

This time Avi smiled as well. "Oh yeah, Tanta Sneakers."

Avi thought of his great-aunt. Though his father didn't like when he called Tanta Hadassah that name, she herself actually enjoyed it. To her it was a name to be proud of and she never stopped the children from addressing her that way. Tanta Hadassah *always* wore sneakers, even on Shabbos. She did this for a very good reason. Tanta Hadassah was always running—running to do *chessed*, of course.

Each day, including Shabbos, she would walk to Burksfield Community Hospital to visit all the sick patients. When she finished there, she would walk all the way to Shaarei Shalom Home for Seniors to spend time visiting and entertaining the lonely, elderly people there. If someone in town was sick, or a woman had a

Mitzvos on Wheels

baby, Tanta Hadassah would run to bring lots of food for the family and treats for the kids. She was such a happy, upbeat person to be around.

When you saw Tanta Hadassah's grey shaitel and big white sneakers stride into the room you just had to smile.

Tanta Hadassah often came to the Drimler home for a Shabbos meal. Her children had all married and moved away and Uncle Reuven had died a couple of years ago. She called herself a "free agent" and was happy to spend time with her Burksfield relatives between running to attend to all her *chessed* obligations. The boys loved it when she spent Shabbos with them.

That night, as the soup was being served, Rabbi Drimler brought up Avi's new project.

"Tanta Hadassah," he began. "I'm proud to tell you that your great-nephew takes after you."

"Really?" Tanta Hadassah glanced at Avi and Shmulie's feet. "I don't see either of these two boys wearing sneakers."

Everyone laughed.

"You know that no one can measure up to your sneakers, Tanta Hadassah!" Rabbi Drimler continued. "But Avi here is giving it a try. Your great-nephew Avi has started his own *chessed* organization."

Avi blushed.

"Really?" asked Tanta Hadassah, turning

The Burksfield Bike Club

to Avi. "What's the name of your organization? What does it do?"

Avi quickly told her all about the Burksfield Bike Club—Mitzvos on Wheels and their "can project."

"Mitzvos on Wheels?" Tanta Hadassah repeated. "I like that name. You know, I have a great *chessed* project that you boys could do. After you finish your 'can' project, of course."

"What's that?" asked Avi.

"Well, many of the old people that I visit in Shaarei Shalom are bored and lonely. Maybe you and your friends could help them find something to do? You know what Chazal say: *Mitzvah goreres mitzvah*—one mitzvah leads to another. Maybe your experience with the 'can project' will help us find a solution to their loneliness."

Shmulie spoke up, bouncing up and down in his seat.

"Yeah, Avi," he said with excitement. "Why don't you give all those old people rides on your bikes?"

At this Avi laughed so hard that the soup in his mouth came pouring out his nose.

Avi imagined himself riding his bike with ninety-year-old Mr. Goldstein sitting on the handlebars.

"What's so funny?" asked Shmulie. "*I* always love riding on the handlebars."

"It's certainly an interesting idea, Shmulie,"

Mitzvos on Wheels

said Tanta Hadassah with a chuckle. "But I don't think old people would enjoy it as much as you."

Avi finished wiping the soup off his face. "I don't think we have time to do anything now, but I'll definitely keep those old people in mind for our next project."

"We're all very proud of you, Avi," his mother joined the conversation as she brought in the next course. "It's beautiful that you want to help Rabbi Goldenberg start his yeshiva. It sounds like a big job, and the harder the job is the bigger the mitzvah."

Avi thought about those words, and he thought about the job ahead of him in the next week. While sitting around the safe, cozy Shabbos table the idea of collecting thousands of cans sounded pretty difficult. He gulped hard.

"What's the matter, Avi?" asked Tanta Hadassah. "You look a little pale."

"Well," Avi stared down at his empty bowl, "I guess I'm a little nervous. We're going to have to collect a lot of cans."

"Hmm," said Tanta Hadassah. "That does sound like a hard job."

"I don't know if we'll be able to do it."

Avi's aunt looked at him determinedly. "That's not your business," she said to her nephew.

"What do you mean?" asked Avi.

"Listen, Avi, the first time I entered a nursing home to do the mitzvah of Bikur Cholim I had no idea what to say to the elderly people I was visiting."

"Were you scared?" asked Shmulie, finally sitting still.

"Oh, very scared," answered Tanta Hadassah. "I was afraid I would not be successful in making anyone feel good at all. I thought I would say something foolish and make all kinds of mistakes."

"What did you do?" asked Avi.

"Well, I realized that being successful was not up to me. It was up to Hashem. I had to do my best and hopefully Hashem would do all the rest," said Tanta Hadassah.

"I think I understand," said Avi. "It's not my business if we get enough cans. That's up to Hashem. We just have to give it our best shot."

"That's right," Tanta Hadassah continued. "Just ask Hashem for help, and do your best."

And with that wise advice the Drimler family continued their meal, doing their best to finish the big job of eating Ima's wonderful dessert.

Sunday morning finally came. The Burksfield Bike Club had all davened at an early minyan so that they could begin to tackle the big job of collecting cans bright and early. They met in front of the shul.

"Okay, guys," Avi said looking around at his friends. "Remember the plan. Just go back to the houses you left flyers at last week. Ring the front bell and ask them for their cans."

"Wait a minute!" Moish cried, slapping his forehead. "We forgot about something."

"What is it, Moish?" asked Eli. He was busy taping a water bottle to one of his handlebars. He had snacks stuffed into a plastic shopping bag that he had tied to the rear of the bike with twist ties. He thought he was pretty well prepared.

"We didn't figure out what to do with the cans once we collect them," Moish looked a little nervous.

"Oh, you're right." As usual Avi was not flustered. A detail like storage space didn't get him rattled. After all, cans weren't slimy and didn't hop around. He had dealt with worse. "It's a good thing you thought about that before we left. Let's go ask Reb Yankel if we can keep the cans in the shul's basement for now."

"Good idea!" said Eli.

The boys left their bikes in front of the shul and went to ask Reb Yankel. They found him in the library rearranging the seforim and approached him respectfully. After some loud throat clearing and serious shuffling by all four boys, Reb Yankel finally turned around.

"Yes?" The *gabbai* peered at them questioningly.

Moish acted as spokesman. "Would Reb Yankel mind if we leave some stuff in the basement for a while?"

"Of course," answered Reb Yankel loudly. "It's a very big mitzvah to smile."

"I don't think he quite understood," Eli muttered softly.

Mitzvos on Wheels

The Burksfield Bike Club

Just then Rabbi Goldenberg appeared. "Of course, boys," he said. He looked sad and distracted. "You can leave whatever you like in the shul's basement. I'm sorry to say that it doesn't look like the basement will be used for anything in the near future anyway."

The boys could see a tear forming on the elderly Rabbi's eye.

"I was hoping to build a yeshiva that would be a fitting memorial for my father, *zt"l*. It's too bad that it won't work out," the Rabbi continued.

All the boys stared down at the ground. What could they possibly say to their aged Rav who looked so sad? Rabbi Goldenberg wiped away the tear and forced himself to smile. He headed toward the basement door, turned on the lights and led the boys downstairs. They followed him down and looked around.

"I'm sorry, boys," Rabbi Goldenberg said taking a deep breath. "I shouldn't be bothering you with my problems. You go on ahead and ride your bikes. The shul will be open all day. You can put anything you like in the basement." With those words, Rabbi Goldenberg walked back upstairs. The boys heard him enter his office and close the door, and then they silently filed out as well.

"Wow!" said Moish. "I never saw Rabbi Goldenberg look so sad."

Mitzvos on Wheels

"I thought I was going to cry," said Eli. Avromy pounded his right fist into his left hand. "We have to do something," he said forcefully.

"We *are* doing something," Avi assured them. "We're going to get on our bikes right now and bring back the cans that will help build Rabbi Goldenberg's yeshiva."

All the boys nodded their heads in agreement.

The elderly Rabbi's tear had been a reminder to them about just how important their project was.

"Good luck everybody!" Avi called. "Let's all try to meet back here by 1:00."

All the boys nodded their heads in agreement, waved, saluted and rode off on their bikes with renewed enthusiasm. They had a mitzvah to do. A very important mitzvah, at that!

Avi felt his stomach doing flip-flops as he walked up the steps to the house of the Silverstein family. For days now he had been picturing this moment over and over again. It had been very easy to imagine it, but doing it in real life really made him nervous. He pictured himself about to dive off of the diving board in the camp pool. It always seemed a little scary, but once he closed his nose and took that jump it turned out to be okay.

Here, he would not be holding his nose. He would be ringing a bell.

"Here goes!" he thought to himself as he closed his eyes and rang the bell. His heart seemed to

Mitzvos on Wheels

pound like a set of bongo drums as he listened for an answer.

There was no answer. Avi actually felt relieved.

"Oh well," he said to himself. "I guess the Silversteins are away. I'll have to come back another time."

He had just begun to turn back towards his bike when he heard the sound of the door opening. Avi quickly turned back towards the door and forced his mouth into a smile.

The door opened all the way and Avi was surprised to see no one in front of him. His heart began to beat faster and louder.

"H-hello?" he stammered into the open doorway.

Suddenly, a voice screamed out "BOO!"

Avi almost jumped six feet into the air. He looked down to see a tiny four-year-old face looking up at him.

"My mommy said to open the door," he said. "Did I scare you?"

"M-m-me? S-s-scared?" Avi stammered. He quickly changed the subject. "Could you tell your mother that I'm here for the cans?"

The boy nodded his head and ran off to the back of the house. Avi tried to remember a kapitel of Tehillim to say. This was not as easy as he thought.

The Burksfield Bike Club

He was suddenly jerked away from his thoughts by another loud "BOO!"

This time Avi really did jump into the air.

The little boy's face was one huge grin. "I really got you that time," he laughed.

Avi noticed that the boy was holding a very heavy looking bag.

"What's that?" he asked This boy was starting to remind him of his kid brother Shmulie and he wanted to speed up this whole exchange and get on to the next house.

"Well, my mommy is on the phone. And I wanted to help her so I put these cans into the bag all by myself. I'm a big mitzvah boy!" He was proud and smiling from ear to ear.

Avi looked into the bag. "These are canned vegetables!" he cried.

"I know," said the boy shaking his head agreeing with Avi's dismay. "I don't really like them either. You can have them all."

"But I don't want canned vegetables!"

"Me neither," said the little boy, "but my mommy says they're good for you."

Avi gave a little groan. Luckily Mrs. Silverstein had gotten off the phone and came to the door.

"Yoni! What are you doing with all my canned vegetables?"

"I wanted to help you, Mommy, so I brought them to this boy for you."

Mitzvos on Wheels

"You want my canned vegetables?" she asked looking down at Avi in surprise.

"N-no," Avi stammered. "I came to collect empty cans for tzedakah. I left a note on your doorstep last week."

"Oh yes," smiled Mrs. Silverstein. "I did get your note. I even prepared a bag of empty cans and bottles for you."

"Thank you very much," Avi replied, breathing a sigh of relief. This conversation had taken a lot of energy!

"Goodbye," called Yoni. "Come back next time and take the vegetables."

A shaken Avi dropped the bag into his bicycle basket and drove off towards the next house.

Once again he held his breath and rang the bell.

"Who is it?" bellowed a voice. It sounded like a rather old man.

"Burksfield Bike Club, can collection!" Avi answered loudly. "I've come to collect your empty bottles and cans."

The door opened and Avi was happy to see a familiar face.

Standing by the door was none other than Milton Greenberg from his shul, Anshei Burksfield. Walking up behind him was his brother Ruby. These eighty year olds were quite a sight. Each of the short, stocky brothers was wear-

The Burksfield Bike Club

ing white shorts and holding a tennis racket.

"How do you like that, Ruby?" Milton called out to his brother. "Those kids really *are* collecting cans for Rabbi Goldenberg's yeshiva."

"I told you, Milton," Ruby looked out over his brother's shoulder. "They really are a swell bunch of kids." He jabbed his brother with his elbow and made a funny face. "They really do everything they *CAN* for the shul."

"I *CAN* understand that," Milton laughed back.

At this, the two elderly brothers began to laugh so hard that tears rolled down their faces.

Avi tried to laugh along, but it wasn't so easy.

"You get it, kid?" Milton nudged Avi. "*CAN!* As in, empty cans!"

Poor Avi managed to chuckle back. He didn't think the joke was all that funny but he didn't want the two men to feel bad.

Suddenly, Milton and Ruby became very serious.

"We have to help them out," rumbled Ruby, rubbing his chin.

"Yeah," agreed Milton, putting down his tennis racket. "We can play tennis anytime. This is a mitzvah."

"Wait here, kid," Ruby motioned to Avi. "We'll get you your cans."

Mitzvos on Wheels

Avi was amazed to watch how fast these two old men could move. They both jogged quickly out of the house and ran down the block together. One went to the house next door and the other went two houses down the street. Avi sat down on their front stoop, watching them as they ran up and down the block.

Meanwhile, only three blocks away, Moish was making his way down Broome Street. At the first three houses he went to nobody answered the door. He was beginning to get frustrated after he came to the fourth house and nobody answered either. Just as he turned away from the door, he heard someone calling him.

"YOO HOO! Young man, come here," came a shrill cry from the side of the house. He recognized Mrs. Blackenstein, the President of the B'nos Burksfield Ladies League. Moish swallowed hard and tried to compose himself. Meeting Mrs. Blackenstein could easily mean time and trouble in his future. Moish jogged over to her.

"Are you here to collect cans for the shul?"

Moish nodded his head in relief.

"Come with me," she said, leading him to the backyard.

Moish was quite surprised at the sight that met his eyes.

In the yard there were two tables lavishly set with all kinds of cakes and cookies. There were

The Burksfield Bike Club

cream puffs and éclairs, *rugalach* and cinnamon buns. Moish even thought he saw a platter of Mrs. Blackenstein's famous chocolate pie. All of Burksfield knew about her super delicious chocolate pie—it was almost as famous as Mrs. Blackenstein herself. About twenty ladies of all ages were laughing and chattering over tea and cake.

Around them were at least twenty-five little children fighting, climbing and jumping on everything in sight.

"We're having our annual B'nos Burksfield Breakfast, where we drink tea while we plan our fundraising Chinese Auction." She didn't say anything about cake.

"That's nice," Moish answered politely.

"Well," said Mrs. Blackenstein, "it would have been nice, except that the girl who was supposed to baby-sit for all our children came down with the flu."

"Oh, that's too bad," said Moish.

"Yes it is," answered Mrs. Blackenstein.

"Here we are trying to arrange a Chinese Auction to raise money for tzedakah and our children are making such a racket."

"That's too bad," Moish said again as he started slowly backing away.

"Yes it is," continued Mrs. Blackenstein confidently. "It would really be terrible if we couldn't

Mitzvos on Wheels

raise money for the poor families in Eretz Yisroel, wouldn't it?"

"Of course," answered Moish, beginning to get very nervous.

"Well," said Mrs. Blackenstein motioning to a pile of bags. "We've all brought our empty bottles and cans for you. Maybe you could help us out as well?"

"H-how?" answered Moish, getting more nervous by the minute.

"I think that you should take these wonderful children with you as you collect all those wonderful cans for tzedakah."

"N-n-no," answered Moish. "I don't think I could do that." Mrs. Blackenstein stared at him coldly.

"You mean you don't want us to raise money for those hungry children in Eretz Yisroel?"

"No!" answered Moish. "I mean, of course I do ... I mean I don't ... I mean I can't really ..."

"Good," answered Mrs. Blackenstein loudly, "then it's settled." She shoved a small plate of chocolate pie at him and turned to gather the children.

"Children! Children! Attention, please!" she yelled at the top of her lungs. "Sari, let go of Aviva's hair. Aaron, get your hands out of the punch. Now everyone line up behind this nice young man. You're going to help him raise money for tzedakah."

Mitzvos on Wheels

Twenty-five voices all shrieked "Yay!" at the same time, except for Aviva who was still screaming "No, No, No!"

Moish groaned from the bottom of his heart. This was turning out to be a very expensive slice of pie.

The smallest of the boys, with the dirtiest of faces, took charge of the group.

"Everybody get into uniform, and meet back here in two minutes!" he shouted.

Moish groaned even louder. "What kind of uniform?"

"We have a club," the little boy said to Moish. "We call ourselves 'The Pot Kids.'"

A few moments later Moish was groaning even louder as twenty-five children lined up behind him. Each wore a pot on his head and held two pot lids in his hands.

"Thank you so much, young man," Mrs. Blackenstein beamed. "Please bring the children back by two."

"Okay, guys!" said the small boy. "Let's make some noise!"

At this, all twenty-five children began clanging their pot lids together, shouting:

"We are the Pot Kids!
We are the Pot Kids!
Give us your cans for tzedakah!"

The Burksfield Bike Club

This time Moish groaned quite loudly, but he couldn't be heard over the clanging of the Pot Kids as they marched along behind him up the block.

• • •

Not too far away Eli rode up the block to the area he had chosen to work on. His first stop was Spruce Street. As he neared the first house, he noticed a big, tall and very hot-looking man pushing a heavy, old lawn mower across the front lawn.

"Good morning!" Eli yelled over the deafening roar of the lawnmower. "I'm here for your cans."

The man wiped some sweat off of his forehead and looked up at Eli.

"What did you say?" he yelled back. The old lawnmower sputtered and clanked under their feet.

Eli yelled back even louder.

"I–SAID–I'M–HERE–FOR–YOUR–CANS!"

The man stared at Eli in amazement. A huge smile broke out across his face.

"YOU SAY YOU WANT TO LEND A HAND?" he yelled. "THAT'S REALLY WONDERFUL! THANKS A LOT."

The smile disappeared instantly from Eli's face. He didn't want to volunteer to schlep a lawnmower. He wanted to collect cans. His mind raced for a way to explain the mistake but the big man grabbed Eli's hand and started shaking it wildly up and down.

"THANK YOU!" he yelled. "THANK YOU SO MUCH! I ALWAYS KNEW THAT YOU YESHIVA BOYS WERE SPECIAL! I HAD NO IDEA THAT YOU WERE *THIS* SPECIAL, THOUGH!"

Eli shrugged his shoulders. Should he explain to the man that he really didn't want to help him do gardening work? Wouldn't that be a *chillul Hashem*? The noise from the lawn mower came to a sudden stop, and then Eli ducked as he saw something flying at him.

"Here," said the smiling man. "Grab this shovel. You can help me with the flowers."

Eli smiled back weakly. The choice seemed clear to him now. He grabbed the shovel and started digging.

The cans would simply have to wait.

On the other side of town Avromy was working up a sweat pedaling from house to house. It really was quite warm, and Avromy wasn't used to doing so much exercise so early in the morning. His first three stops had gone well. Those families had bags of empty bottles and cans waiting for him when he came. The fourth house on the block, however, was a bit scary for Avromy. The house was quite large. Some might even have called it a mansion. Nowadays, though, it certainly didn't look like a wealthy person owned it. The paint was peeling off every inch of its outer walls. The front lawn was like a forest of overgrown weeds and

Mitzvos on Wheels

The Burksfield Bike Club

bushes. It looked dark and dreary even in the morning sunshine.

This was Max Feingold's house. Everyone in Burksfield had heard the name, but few people had ever seen the man. It was well known that he had once been fabulously wealthy. As he got older, Max sold his business and closed himself up in his house. Avromy saw him twice a year. On Rosh Hashanah and Yom Kippur, Max would come to Anshei Burksfield. He sat in the back of the shul and would hardly say a word to anyone. He wore a very old-looking grey suit with a tiny red bow tie. If you wished him a "Good Yom Tov," he would just nod his head and grunt in return. Avromy didn't think it would be easy to get cans from a man like Max Feingold. But Avromy was a super salesman and he loved a challenge! He would find a way to talk Max into giving him something for the new yeshiva, no matter how hard it would be.

He walked up the front steps, took a deep breath, and rang the bell. A shiver went up Avromy's back. Instead of a gentle ring, the bell produced a loud squawking sound. It sounded like a duck swallowing a basketball.

He felt a cold shivery feeling and quickly looked up. An eye was peeking out at him from an ancient, dust-covered peephole in the door. He took a deep breath and got himself ready. The door creaked loudly as it swung open.

Mitzvos on Wheels

Standing in the entranceway was old Max Feingold, wearing the same old grey suit and red bow tie that he wore on Rosh Hashanah.

"H-h-hello, Mr. Feingold," Avromy stammered nervously.

Mr. Feingold sternly stared down at the nervous boy.

"Aren't you Lester Froob's son?" he boomed.

"Y-yes, I am," Avromy answered a little more confidently. Maybe if Mr. Feingold remembered him from Anshei Burksfield he would be more inclined to help out. He noticed that Mr. Feingold kept looking up and down the street behind him. Mr. Feingold actually seemed nervous that someone might see him.

"I know why you're here," he said to Avromy as his eyes scanned the street.

"You do?" asked Avromy, picking up his head a bit. Maybe this would be easier than he thought.

"Of course I do," said Mr. Feingold. "You're here for my treasure."

"That's right, Mr. Feingold," Avromy began with a smile. "I came to pick up all of your ca—" Avromy stopped in mid-sentence, his smile disappearing in a flash. "Did you say *treasure*?" he asked, reaching to clean out his right ear.

"*Shhh!*" hissed Mr. Feingold loudly. "People

might hear you. Do you want *them* to come after my treasure?"

"Er ... I guess not," Avromy answered, not really knowing what to say. He thought about it and looked at Mr. Feingold carefully.

"Umm ... Mr. Feingold?" he began timidly. "Would ... umm ... would you let *me* see your treasure?"

"*You?*" asked Mr. Feingold in astonishment.

Avromy looked around the street.

"Uh ... yes ... me," he answered.

Mr. Feingold looked at him suspiciously.

"Are you sure you're Lester Froob's son?"

"Yes, I am," answered Avromy. This was one thing he was absolutely sure of.

"Hmmm," said Mr. Feingold. Avromy could almost hear Mr. Feingold's thoughts as they rattled around in his head. "Isn't your father the one that sold me my refrigerator?"

"That's probably true, Mr. Feingold," said Avromy proudly. "My father sells lots of refrigerators."

"Hmmm," said the old man thoughtfully. "I like that refrigerator, you know."

Avromy smiled. "I'm happy to hear that. They say that Froob's Fantastic Fridges is the best refrigerator store around."

"Well," said Mr. Feingold, "if your father sold me such a good refrigerator, I guess I can trust you."

"Of course!" said Avromy, nodding his head

Mitzvos on Wheels

vigorously. Even though he was not quite sure what Mr. Feingold was talking about, he tried to look like he knew what was going on.

"Follow me," said Mr. Feingold as he stepped outside and started to walk around the side of his house. "But don't tell anyone what you saw."

"*Bli neder*, I won't," answered Avromy excitedly. He had never seen a real treasure before. He wondered what it looked like.

Mr. Feingold walked to a gate in the tall fence surrounding the sides of his house. Avromy's stomach did a couple of somersaults as he watched the old man slowly turn the key in an old rusty lock. Mr. Feingold kept looking from side to side to see if there were any snooping neighbors or other people passing by.

The door creaked open. Mr. Feingold turned to Avromy.

"Look!" he whispered. "Come look at my beautiful treasure."

Avromy was shaking with excitement as he peered in through the open door. He had imagined he would see gold and diamonds piled to the sky.

What he did see really surprised him. Before him stood a large yard full of piles and piles of ... junk! There were stacks, heaps and mounds of all kinds of thrown out stuff. There was a ten-foot-tall pile of old newspapers. A five-foot-high

The Burksfield Bike Club

pile of bicycle tires. A huge jumble of old rusty doll strollers. Any kind of junk you could dream of lay scattered across the whole yard; under trees, behind bushes, and even piled up against the gate.

Avromy scanned the yard in amazement. Then he saw something that made his heart jump. In the center of the yard was an old swimming pool. It looked like it had not been used in decades. It was bone dry and filled with something far more precious than water.

It was full of empty cans and bottles!

Avromy's mind raced. He was a good salesman, but would he be able to talk Mr. Feingold into giving him some of his treasure?

Avromy turned to Mr. Feingold with his widest salesman smile. He cleared his throat and stood a little straighter.

"Mr. Feingold," he began softly. "Do you know Rabbi Goldenberg?"

"Of course I do," the old man answered with great respect. "I knew his father as well. I would do anything for a great man like Rabbi Goldenberg."

Avromy almost did a cartwheel for joy. It was a done deal! There was no doubt in his mind that he would get Mr. Feingold to donate that pile of cans. A little talk, some reminiscing, and Mr. Feingold would surely be sharing

Mitzvos on Wheels

his "treasures." His only worry now would be how to get it back to the shul.

"May I sit down, Mr. Feingold? I would love to hear all about Rabbi Goldenberg's father and how things were before I was born."

• • •

Back on Spruce Street Eli was not having much luck. He was dripping with sweat and covered with dirt. He had planted two rows of petunias and then spent half an hour weeding around them. The roses were beautiful as well, but he preferred to see them cut and sitting in a vase on his mother's Shabbos table.

Mr. Applebaum, the owner of the garden, could not stop talking about how wonderful Eli and all yeshiva boys were. He was so impressed at Eli for volunteering to help him.

"You know, son," he said, "I can't thank you enough for helping me today. I love my garden and I just can't seem to find the help I need to keep it up. There's nothing that gives me more pleasure than sitting on a lawn chair in my beautiful, colorful garden and enjoying the outdoors. What can I do to thank you? Is there anything I can give you as a reward?"

"Well," said Eli, wiping sweat off his brow, "I could use some empty cans."

The Burksfield Bike Club

"*Empty cans?*" asked Mr. Applebaum in amazement. "Why would you want empty cans?"

"Well," answered Eli, "my Rabbi wants to build a new yeshiva, and my friends and I are collecting empty cans to raise money for it."

"A new yeshiva?" asked the man in amazement. "You mean a school that will produce fine young men like you? That's just great!"

Eli's face turned red. "Er ... thank you," he stammered. He didn't know how being a good gardener made him such a "fine young man," but he was glad he had made a *kiddush Hashem.*

A large smile broke out across Mr. Applebaum's face. "I can get you some cans," he said.

"Oh, thank you," said Eli again. He was anxious to get moving. *At least I'll get a few cans today*, he thought to himself.

"Have you ever heard of Apple Supermarket?" asked Mr. Applebaum.

"Of course I have," answered Eli. "My mother shops there all the time."

"Well, the name Apple is really short for Applebaum."

Eli looked up at the man in amazement. "That's *your* store?" he asked.

"That's right, and I've got a whole storeroom full of empty cans that I would love to donate to

Mitzvos on Wheels

your new yeshiva! The man reached for his car keys. "Get on your bike and meet me in front of my store. I'll be there in a few minutes and set you up with cans galore!"

Eli thought he would faint! He dropped the gardening gloves Mr. Applebaum had given him, brushed off his dirty pants and ran for his bike. *Wow!* Eli thought to himself, *it looks like planting petunias got me some cans after all!*

Larry Rosenberg paced up and down Main Street, a nervous wreck. Being chief photographer for the *Burksfield Bugle* was not an easy job. True, the Bugle was a small newspaper that only came out once a week, but that didn't matter to Larry's boss, Mr. Jonathan Tate. Tate was very demanding and ran his newspaper as if it was a national daily. When he wanted something done it had to be done immediately, or else! Poor Larry had until the end of the day to find an interesting picture for the *Bugle*'s front page. He shuddered to think of Tate's reaction if he didn't find one.

Larry wrung his hands. Burksfield was such a small, quiet town. Nothing exciting

Mitzvos on Wheels

ever happened here. What could possibly be interesting enough for him to snap a picture of?

From inside his pocket came the familiar ring of his cell phone. It was his wife Sarah. "Did you get a picture yet?" she asked, hopefully. "Do you think you'll be home soon?"

"Are you kidding?" he almost yelled into the phone. "At this rate, I'll be home next week! Nothing interesting ever happens here."

Not too far away, Avromy was huffing and puffing as he pedaled his bike towards shul. It hadn't been easy to convince Max Feingold to give up any of his "treasure," but Avromy's smooth talking had convinced him that mitzvos were a much greater treasure than cans. Mr. Feingold had even agreed to lend Avromy some more of his treasures to hold the cans in.

Sweat poured down his face as he turned to look at the six rusty old baby carriages tied to the back of his bike. Avromy realized that his little train of cans looked very silly. He was also a little embarrassed by the bag of cans he was balancing on his head.

"Oh well," he said to himself. "It's for a mitzvah, and besides no one seems to be noticing me anyway."

Up the street, Larry continued ranting into his phone.

65

The Burksfield Bike Club

"I tell you, Sarah," he screamed in frustration, "Burksfield is the most boring place on earth! Other towns have exciting things going on. Here, I look up the street and see nothing—just a kid on a bike balancing a bag on his head, pulling six baby carriages full of old cans. Could it get any more boring?

"And behind the kid is a parade. It's like I said, Sarah," he screamed, "nothing interesting *ever* happ—" Suddenly, Larry dropped his phone.

"A *parade*? I don't believe what I see!" he said, rubbing his eyes.

Larry took one more look, picked up his battered cell phone from the ground, gripped his camera and began running down the street.

Mitzvos on Wheels

Avi was having a lot of fun. He was sitting in the back seat of Milton and Ruby's antique convertible car. The roof had been rolled down and a nice cool breeze was blowing in his face. Avi chuckled to himself as he looked at the Burksfield Bike Club parade that had formed. In front of his car was Moish, marching with a large group of kids with pots on their heads. They were making quite a racket, clanging pot lids and shaking bags of cans as they walked. In front of them was Avromy, pulling six old baby carriages full of cans.

Milton and Ruby were also having a great time waving to all the people they passed.

Mitzvos on Wheels

Milton pressed a button and a loud "tootle-de-toot" rang out from under the old car's hood. Both men laughed out loud.

Suddenly, they heard a loud sound that made them all jump up in their seats. An extremely loud *Honkkkk* and the roar of an engine came from behind them. Avi quickly turned around and his mouth dropped open. Behind him was a huge white truck, and Eli was sitting in the front seat waving wildly and grinning from ear to ear. He held up an empty soda can with one hand and pointed to the back of the truck with the other.

Mr. Applebaum winked at Eli and stuck his head out the window.

"We got lots of cans for the yeshiva," he yelled, smiling.

As the parade traveled, more and more curious people gathered to watch. No one could figure out what was going on. By the time they reached Anshei Burksfield, an impressive crowd had gathered. Eli jumped out of the truck and ran to Avi.

"Is that truck full of what I think it is?" Avi asked Eli.

"You bet!" answered Eli. "Mr. Applebaum has generously donated a truckload of cans."

"Wow! Let's get them off the truck."

By this time all of the Burksfield Bike Club had gathered together. In no time at all the boys pulled ten huge sacks of cans off the truck.

The Burksfield Bike Club

"Good luck, boys!" called Mr. Applebaum as he drove off.

"Okay," said Avi. "Now let's get *all* of the cans down into the shul's basement."

It took some schlepping, but in a short time every last can was safely inside.

"I got lots of cans from Mr. Feingold," huffed Avromy, trying to catch his breath.

"Well," said Moish, "these kids and I got a nice amount of cans, too. Hey, pot kids," he yelled at his group, "how many cans do we have all together?"

In unison, twenty-five children with pots on their heads all screamed out:

"We are the pot kids,
we got three hundred and two cans.
We are the pot kids,
we got three hundred and two cans."

Everyone held their ears until they had finished. The boys then helped Avromy count all the cans he had brought. Avi pulled out a calculator and furiously began to punch in numbers.

"Listen everyone!" he shouted. "We have a total of two thousand, two hundred cans!"

"Hooray!"

"Yippee!"

"Wow!"

Mitzvos on Wheels

"That's great!"

Avi punched in some more numbers.

"If each can is worth five cents, that would give us a total of—"

"I bet it's at least five hundred dollars," said Eli, jumping up and down.

"Nu?" yelled Moish. "Tell us already! How much money did we raise for the yeshiva?"

Avi motioned for quiet as he punched in the last numbers.

"That gives us a total of one hundred and ten dollars."

The pot kids began jumping up and down slapping each other on the back. "Yay!" they yelled.

"A hundred and ten dollars?" screamed the leader of the pot kids. "That's *so* much money."

"Yeah," said another pot kid, "it's almost like a million dollars."

"Even more," said the leader, "it's like *a thousand* dollars!"

"*Ooooh!*" cheered all his friends.

The boys from the Burksfield Bike Club, however, did not look as happy. Their heads hung low.

"All that work for one hundred and ten dollars?" asked Avromy sadly.

"Yeah, I thought it would be a lot more," said Eli.

"Rabbi Goldenberg needs *twenty-thousand* dollars to open his yeshiva," said Moish. "One hundred and ten is like nothing."

Mitzvos on Wheels

Avi looked as though he were about to cry. He had really thought that their hard work would bring in a lot more money. Tears began to form in the corners of his eyes. Then, from behind, he felt a warm, firm hand on his shoulder.

"I don't believe it," said a soft, familiar voice. Avi whirled around to find Rabbi Goldenberg standing behind him. His face was glowing with happiness.

"I just don't believe it," said the elderly Rabbi. "I am amazed at how hard you boys worked to raise money for the yeshiva."

He walked around the room and placed a loving kiss on each boy's head.

"You should just know," he said, "that this morning I had decided to give up on the idea for the yeshiva."

"You did?" asked Avi.

"Yes," said Rabbi Goldenberg. "I thought that it would be impossible to raise the money I need. But you boys showed me that a Jew should never give up, no matter how hard things seem to be."

The members of the Burksfield Bike Club looked at one another, and slowly each face exchanged its gloomy look for a happier one. The peaceful look on their Rabbi's face made them feel very proud.

"What are you going to do, Rabbi Goldenberg?" asked Moish.

The Burksfield Bike Club

"What am I going to do?" said the Rabbi with a smile. "I'll do what every Jew does when he needs help. I'll daven!"

Everyone in the room smiled.

"We'll daven, too," said Avi.

"*And* we'll get more cans," added Eli.

"That's wonderful," said Rabbi Goldenberg. "We all need to do our best, and then ask Hashem to do the rest." He held out his hands gently as he spoke, waved goodbye and slowly shuffled his way back upstairs.

Where have I heard those words before? Avi asked himself. *Oh yeah! That's exactly what Tanta Hadassah told me on Shabbos.* "I guess we have to get back to work," he said aloud.

"How many more cans can we possibly get?" asked Moish. "It'll probably take half a million to make twenty thousand dollars."

"That's a good point," said Avi glumly.

"Mincha!" called Rabbi Drimler from the top of the basement stairs.

"You know what?" said Avi. "Let's do what Rabbi Goldenberg said. Let's daven for it. We'll meet here again tomorrow after camp."

The boys all nodded their heads in agreement and walked towards the staircase. Right now things seemed very overwhelming. Davening sounded like the best thing to do.

That night, Avi went to bed in a pretty unhappy mood. He kept tossing and turning from side to side. One question kept rolling around his head: How would they ever be able to raise enough money for the yeshiva?

Every time he *did* manage to fall asleep, he dreamt about one thing—*cans*! In one dream he was being buried under a mountain of cans. In another dream, a humongous can with sharp metal teeth was chasing him down the street. After each nightmare he woke up in a cold sweat, his heart pounding wildly.

By the time morning came, Avi was happy to leave his bed. He did not feel rested at all.

The Burksfield Bike Club

Slowly, he washed *negel vasser* and pulled himself out of bed. He was just starting to convince himself to get dressed when a loud banging on his bedroom door interrupted him.

"Avi," called his mother. "Quickly, get dressed and come downstairs. You're not going to believe what I have to show you."

"What's going on?" asked Avi sleepily.

"Just get dressed and come down," called Mrs. Drimler. "You'll see."

Avi quickly pulled his clothing on and ran downstairs to the kitchen. His whole family was sitting around the table reading something. "What's that?" he asked anxiously.

Avi's father stood up. "This," he said, waving a newspaper in Avi's face, "is a copy of the latest edition of the *Burksfield Bugle*. Why don't you take a look at the front page?"

Avi took the paper from his father. His whole family stood smiling around him as he unfolded the newspaper.

"Wow," said Shmulie. "Avi's eyes are as big as Frisbees."

Everyone laughed except for Avi. He was too busy staring at the most incredible thing he had ever seen.

Spread out in front of him was the front page of the newspaper with a headline that read: "CAN PARADE ON MAIN STREET."

Mitzvos on Wheels

The Burksfield Bike Club

Beneath that was a huge picture of himself and his friends. In front was a very sweaty Avromy, pedaling his bike and balancing a bag of cans on his head. Moish followed behind him, with the pot kids holding their cans. Very clearly behind them was Avi, sitting next to Milton and Ruby in their car. In the background was a large truck with a boy in its front window waving.

"I don't believe it," Avi mumbled to himself. He stared at the newspaper as if it would disappear in an instant. Just then the phone rang.

"It's Tanta Ida on the phone," Rabbi Drimler told everyone. "It seems she saw Avi's picture in the paper."

"My cousin Bracha already called half an hour ago," added Mrs. Drimler.

Avi hardly heard them. He just kept staring at the newspaper saying "wow" to himself over and over again.

"Come on, Avi," said Shmulie. "Read me what it says."

Avi realized that there was a written paragraph under the picture as well. He began to read out loud:

> "*Our quiet town of Burksfield was abuzz with activity yesterday. A parade was spotted marching down Main Street early Sunday afternoon. Burksfield's oldest*

Mitzvos on Wheels

synagogue, Anshei Burksfield, is planning on opening a yeshiva (a school for Jewish boys) in its basement. The boys in the above photo began an empty can collection drive to raise funds for the project."

"*RINGG!*" The phone rang again.

"Avi," said Mrs. Drimler, "Tanta Hadassah wants to speak to you."

"Well, hello, Avi." Tanta Hadassah's voice came across strong and clear over the phone. "I saw your picture in the paper. I'm very proud of your good work for tzedakah."

"Thank you, Tanta Hadassah," said Avi. "You should just know that Rabbi Goldenberg said the exact same words you told me. He said that a Jew has to do his best, and ask Hashem to do the rest."

"Well, I'm happy to hear that. By the way, since you remember my words so well, I'll remind you that I need your help finding something for the people in Shaarei Shalom to do."

"I remember what you said," said Avi. "*Mitzvah goreres mitzvah.*"

"That's right," said his aunt. "So when you have a chance, please think about it."

"I will, *bli neder*. Whoops! It's late, and I need to get to camp."

"Have a good day, Avi."

The Burksfield Bike Club

"Goodbye, Tanta," said Avi, hanging up the phone.

"Avi," Rabbi Drimler stopped him, "I heard you mention *mitzvah goreres mitzvah* on the phone. I just want you to know that I spoke to Mrs. Berkowitz on the phone this morning."

"That's nice," said Avi. "Er ... who's Mrs. Berkowitz? And what does that have to do with *mitzvah goreres mitzvah*?"

"She's a very nice lady who says that her dog Blacky is a good friend of yours."

"Oh," Avi laughed. "Blacky's owner."

"That's right," said Rabbi Drimler, "and tonight she and her husband Mike are going to start coming to classes to learn more about *Yiddishkeit*."

"Wow!" Avi felt like jumping into the air. "That's great!"

"Also," continued Rabbi Drimler, "I saw how happy Rabbi Goldenberg was by Mincha yesterday. I think *you* put that smile there. That's another mitzvah."

Avi blushed.

"Keep it up, Avi," said his father. "It looks like you've really started a whole chain of mitzvos."

• • •

A very happy Avi hopped onto his bike and pedaled off to camp that morning. He walked

Mitzvos on Wheels

into his learning group a little late and was embarrassed to find twenty pairs of eyes immediately focused upon him. Instead of looking into their seforim, every single boy in the room was staring intently at Avi with big smiles on their faces. Avromy, Eli and Moish were also smiling widely; they looked like their faces would burst!

"Okay, everyone," said Rabbi Silver. "I know a celebrity has just walked in, but our job is to learn Torah. You'll be able to talk to Avi later."

All eyes immediately turned back to the open *gemaras*.

Avi tried to focus on the page in front of him, but it was so hard. He could almost *hear* the *yetzer hara*'s voice screaming at him to stop learning and think about the newspaper article.

He tried to imagine himself punching the *yetzer hara* out of his mind, but then he realized that that was exactly what the *yetzer hara* wanted him to do—to think about anything else except for the *gemara* in front of him. When Rebbe asked for a volunteer to say the *gemara*, Avi was the first to raise his hand. He knew he couldn't daydream if he was reading out loud in front of the whole class. He started saying over the *gemara*, but soon Rebbe stopped him to ask another student a question.

The Burksfield Bike Club

"Eli," he said, "why does Rav disagree with Shmuel?"

Eli looked like he had just swallowed a porcupine.

"Er ..." he stammered, "because of the cans in the Mishnah?"

The whole bunk laughed. Eli blushed. It was quite obvious what he had been thinking about during learning.

"I know it's hard right now, Eli," said Rabbi Silver gently, "but please try your best to pay attention."

"Yes, Rebbe," Eli stammered. From that time on he really did try hard to focus on the *gemara*. When learning groups ended, Avi, Eli, Avromy and Moish were surrounded by every other boy in their bunk.

"I saw you in the newspaper!" yelled one excited boy.

"Was that Eli in the truck?" asked another.

"Who's old car was Avi in?" asked someone else.

The boys from the Burksfield Bike Club very much wanted to talk to each other, but no one would give them the chance. Their friends had lots of questions and wouldn't leave them alone until they were answered.

Finally, everything was explained down to the last detail. The last "I can't believe it!" and

Mitzvos on Wheels

"Boy, you guys are lucky!" rang through the air. The counselors showed up and started organizing a ball game and the Burksfield Bike Club was finally able to slip away.

"Whew!" said Avromy, wiping his forehead. "I'm glad that's over."

"Yeah," agreed Moish.

"What are we going to do next?" asked Eli, turning to Avi.

"Well," said Avi, "we finally answered everyone else's questions, but we still have lots of questions ourselves."

"Yeah," said Moish, "like what will we do after camp today?"

"That's simple," said Avromy. "We go back to collecting cans from people's houses."

"You want to do that *again*?" Moish looked dejected.

"Yeah," said Eli, "we worked *so* hard yesterday, and got *so* little."

"No!" Avi was firm. "We can't think like that. Avromy is right. We *have* to go back to can collecting. Remember what Rabbi Goldenberg said. We have to do our best and ask Hashem to do the rest."

"But we did our best already," Moish pointed out.

"Yeah, but who knows what could happen today?" said Avi.

The Burksfield Bike Club

"That's right," Avromy agreed. "We won't get *anything* for the yeshiva if we don't try."

The boys were interrupted by shouts from behind them. It was Shimmy their counselor.

"Come on, you guys," he called. "We need you for the baseball game. Everyone is waiting."

After camp the boys met once again. They stood around leaning on their bikes and had a conference.

"Okay," said Avi, "let's try it again. It's not Sunday today, so we won't have *that* much time, but who knows *what* Hashem will send our way."

"That's right," said Avromy, "let's meet back at the shul in two hours."

The boys were about to split up when they heard voices calling.

"Wait, wait!" came the shouts.

They looked up the block and saw the other nine boys from their bunk riding over on their bikes.

The Burksfield Bike Club

"Can we help you today?" asked Yitzy Zarf.

The members of the Burksfield Bike Club looked at each other in confusion.

"You want to help us?" asked Avi in disbelief. Avi and the other boys were not looking forward to another round of can collecting. They couldn't believe that anyone else would either.

"Please!" begged Akiva Green. "Just for the next few days."

"Excuse us a minute," said Avi politely.

Avi, Moish, Avromy and Eli huddled together to discuss the new events.

"What do you think, guys?" asked Avi. "Should we let them help us today?"

"I don't know," said Avromy. "This was *our* project."

"That's right," agreed Eli. "Why should we give away our mitzvah?"

"They wouldn't be taking our mitzvah away," cried Moish. "They would be giving us a *bigger* mitzvah."

"What do you mean?" asked Eli.

"It's simple," said Moish. "The more guys we have collecting, the more cans we can collect, and the more money we raise for Rabbi Goldenberg's yeshiva."

"Not only that," Avi continued for him, "we will also get the mitzvah of helping the other boys get a mitzvah. *Mitzvah goreres mitzvah.*"

Mitzvos on Wheels

"I get what you're saying," said Avromy, nodding his head.

The boys looked back at their bunkmates who waited anxiously for their decision. "Let's take a vote," said Avi. "All those in favor of letting them help, raise your hand."

Four hands went up. Everyone smiled.

"YOU CAN HELP!" they yelled to their friends together.

The nine other boys returned their smiles happily and pulled up their bikes to get their instructions. The newcomers were quickly told where to go and what to say. In no time at all, thirteen bikes were riding through Burksfield, all on a mitzvah mission.

• • •

Two hours later, thirteen very exhausted bike riders pulled up in front of Anshei Burksfield. On this day, there were no truckloads of cans, only bags full. They had only enough time to put them into the shul's basement before it was time to daven Mincha.

"We'll meet here again after camp tomorrow," said Avi. "You guys can come, too," he said motioning to the new boys.

Sure enough, the next day the boys all found themselves once again standing in front of Anshei Burksfield with bags of cans hanging from their bicycles.

"I'm getting tired of this," complained Moish. "Are we really accomplishing anything by schlepping around every afternoon?"

Avi swung open the door to the basement.

"Look!" He pointed to the growing pile of cans in the center of the floor. "Each one of those means we are five cents closer to building a yeshiva. Of course we have to keep collecting."

"Okay," said Moish, "maybe you're right. Maybe we should keep collecting. But what are we going to *do* with all these cans anyway? Who is going to *give* us the five cents for each of them?"

"Whoops!" said Avi, slapping his forehead. "We never thought about that!"

"Oh, don't worry," said Eli. "I know exactly what we have to do."

"You do?" asked the other boys in amazement.

"Of course I do," answered Eli. "It's a piece of cake. Mr. Applebaum explained it all to me while we were riding in his truck."

The boys looked at him and waited for more of an explanation.

"Mr. Applebaum and I spoke about it in his truck that day," repeated Eli. "Like I said, it's a piece of cake. First we have to wash the cans to

Mitzvos on Wheels

make sure they're clean. Then we have to sort them into three piles—one pile for each soda company. After that, all we have to do is call the companies to come pick up the cans."

The boys stood staring at Eli in disbelief.

"That's what you call a piece of cake?" shouted Moish. "What kind of cake do they eat in your house? Is it made of iron?"

All the boys stared at the pile of cans in the center of the room. It seemed to be growing larger by the minute.

"That does sound like an awful lot of work," said Avromy.

"It sounds like it could take us a whole week just to get *these* cans ready," groaned Moish.

"You know, you're right," admitted Eli. "It sounded a lot simpler when Mr. Applebaum explained it to me."

"What do we do now?" asked Moish. "It looks like we didn't accomplish anything by all our collecting."

Once again the boys found themselves feeling hopeless and discouraged as they stood staring at the cans in their shul's basement. Once again, Avi felt tears forming in his eyes.

Then, for the second time in a week, he felt a familiar hand on his shoulder.

"I don't believe it!" came the gentle voice of Rabbi Goldenberg.

Mitzvos on Wheels

The boys whirled around to find their elderly rabbi standing behind them once again. This time his smile seemed even larger than before. They noticed one thing strange and different, though. It was a large shopping bag hanging from his hand.

"Oh, there are more of you now," he said. "That's wonderful!"

Once again he walked around the room planting kisses on each boy's head.

"And do you boys know what is in this bag?" he asked, grinning from ear to ear.

The boys all looked at each other and shrugged their shoulders.

"Er ... no, we don't," answered Avi.

Rabbi Goldenberg stuck his hand into the bag and pulled out a thick pile of envelopes.

"Look!" he cried excitedly. "Look at these." He held out the bag for them to look inside.

"These," cried the old Rabbi hoarsely, "are checks people mailed to me. They read about you boys in the newspaper and they want to help build the new yeshiva. There must be at least thirty checks in here. All because of you boys and your can collection."

"Wow!"

"I can't believe it!"

"Who would have thought?"

Twelve boys smiled wildly and some turned towards Moish.

"Okay," admitted Moish raising his hands in defeat. "Maybe I was wrong. Maybe we *did* accomplish something with our collecting."

All the boys laughed.

"Did we make a *lot* of money?" asked Avromy.

"Well," said Rabbi Goldenberg, "most of the checks are for eighteen or twenty-five dollars, but added together that comes out to a nice amount of money."

"Not twenty thousand dollars, though …" remarked Moish hesitantly.

"Well," said Rabbi Goldenberg, "that's why we have to keep davening."

"And collecting," added Avi.

"That's right," continued Rabbi Goldenberg. "We have to make our *hishtadlus*, to show Hashem we are trying our best."

"And ask him to do the rest," added Avi with a smile.

"Thank you, boys," said Rabbi Goldenberg heading for the door, "and keep it up."

For a few moments after the door closed, there was complete silence in the shul basement. The boys basked in the warm glow of the smile and kiss the Rabbi had just given them. They thought about all that had happened and how one never knew how things would turn out.

Suddenly, Moish broke the silence.

"Uh oh!" he said loudly. "It's happening again."

"What's happening?" asked Yechiel anxiously.

"Oh no!" added Avromy. "I see it, too!"

"What are you guys talking about?" asked Yitzy Zarf.

"Look!" said Moish pointing at Avi. His eyes were crinkled up in just that special way and his eyebrows turned down as he stared distractedly into space.

"Why is everybody staring at me?" asked Avi with a startled look.

"You've got that look in your eye again," Eli announced.

"Okay, tell us Avi," Avromy spoke for them all. "Does your plan have anything to do with getting these cans cleaned and sorted?"

"Are you guys reading my mind again?" asked Avi, eyes wide in disbelief.

"Well," said Moish, "you do you have a plan, don't you?"

"As a matter of fact," said Avi with a thoughtful smile on his face, "I do."

"Are we going to sell Jewish soda cans this time instead of Jewish frogs?" teased Eli. "I think they would look great with little pairs of tzitzis on them."

"No, no!" said Avi, stroking his chin. He was too lost in thought to get annoyed. "This plan is *gevaldik*! It's unbelievable! It's perfect!"

The Burksfield Bike Club

"What? What? Tell us already," cried Avromy. "I'm dying to know. What's the plan?"

"It's very simple," said Avi. "The plan is ... *mitzvah goreres mitzvah.*"

"Huh?"

"What?"

"C'mon, Avi, explain!"

Avi quickly ran for the door. "Quick guys!" he yelled, "hop on your bikes and follow me!"

"Where are we going?" huffed Avromy running out the door.

"You'll see," said Avi. "It's going to be great!"

Twelve confused boys jumped onto their bikes and followed Avi.

"I don't know what's gotten into Avi," panted Moish to Eli. "Look at him, he's got the strangest look in his eyes."

"Yeah," agreed Eli, "and look how he's smiling. You would think he just won the lottery or something."

"Boy," huffed Avromy, sweat pouring down his face. "I've gotten more exercise in the last week than I got the whole last year. I hope Avi's making us rush like this for a good reason."

After ten minutes of riding, the boys found themselves pedaling into the driveway of

The Burksfield Bike Club

Shaarei Shalom Home for Seniors.

"What in the world are we doing here?" panted Avromy, trying to catch his breath.

"This," said Avi triumphantly, "is an example of *mitzvah goreres mitzvah*."

"It looks like an old age home to me," said Eli, wiping the sweat off his face.

The other boys shook their heads in agreement.

"Listen, guys ..." cried Avi. "My Tanta Sneaker ... I mean, my Tanta Hadassah Goodside spends a lot of time visiting with the old people who live here."

"That's nice," said Moish, "but what does that have to do with our cans?"

"Well," continued Avi patiently, "my aunt is always telling me that the old people who live here are bored and need things to keep them busy and feeling useful."

"Are you thinking what I think you're thinking?" asked Avromy slowly.

Avi was so excited he was jumping up and down.

"Yes!" he shouted. "We can ask the people in Shaarei Shalom to clean and sort the bottles for us! It will be two mitzvos at the same time. The yeshiva will get the money from the bottles, and the older people will have an important job to keep them busy."

"Oh," said Eli, "that's what you meant by *mitzvah goreres mitzvah*."

"Exactly."

"What a great idea," said Moish. "This really *is* a great plan, Avi."

"Okay," Avi pulled off his bike helmet and directed everyone. "Let's park our bikes behind the building and go inside. My Tanta Hadassah should be here now. I'm sure she'll be very happy with this plan."

The boys parked their bikes and walked into the building. As soon as they entered the front door, a Chinese lady holding a clipboard came running over to them.

"Are you here for Hadassah Goodside?" she asked frantically.

"Er ... yes, we are," answered Avi nervously. "How did you know?"

"Are you from the day camp?" she asked.

"Yeah," said Avi shrugging his shoulders. "We left camp not too long ago."

"That's great!" cried the lady. "Follow me!"

She began to race down the hall, motioning for the boys to follow her.

"Oh great!" huffed Avromy. "First we race on bikes and now we race in halls. I can hardly breathe."

"Let me introduce myself," said the lady as she flew down the hall. "My name is Nancy Chin, and I am the entertainment director for Shaarei Shalom."

The boys all nodded their heads as they ran.

The Burksfield Bike Club

"Where are we running to?" Moish whispered to Avi.

"Beats me," answered Avi. "I guess she's bringing us to my aunt."

They came to a door at the end of a hallway and suddenly Nancy Chin stopped.

"Okay," she said motioning toward the door, "go in."

A very confused bunch of boys began walking through the doorway into a dark room.

"What is this place, Avi?" asked Moish. "Why does your aunt work in such a dark room?"

Mrs. Chin closed the door behind them and the boys found themselves in complete darkness.

"Hey!" yelled Avi. "What's going on?"

All the boys were very frightened. They could not figure out what was happening.

Suddenly, they heard a familiar Chinese voice speaking into a microphone.

"And now," she said very dramatically, "we are proud to present some wonderful entertainment to the residents of Shaarei Shalom."

"What's she talking about?" whispered Eli in the darkness.

Mrs. Chin continued in a loud voice.

"To sing for you today, we have brought members of CAMP BAIS YAAKOV!"

The boys heard clapping and felt the swish of a curtain opening in front of them.

Mitzvos on Wheels

When the curtain opened the boys almost fainted.

They were standing on a stage! In front of them were about a hundred old men and women. All the residents of Shaarei Shalom home for Senior Citizens were sitting and staring at ... *them*!

They gazed at their audience speechlessly. Their audience stared back at them. Nancy Chin came running over to the foot of the stage.

"Come on, boys," she whispered frantically. "Start singing!"

"Dot's Bais Yaakov Kemp?" cried an old lady in the front row. "I didn't know they had boychiks in de Bais Yaakov Kemp!"

"*Bais Yaakov camp?*" hissed Moish. "What's she talking about?"

"Come on, boys," cried Nancy. "Sing already!"

"But ... but ..." stammered Avi, "... we're not Bais Yaakov Camp."

Nancy Chin looked like she was about to have a nervous breakdown.

"I don't care who you are," she cried, pulling at her hair. "Just start singing!"

The boys shuffled nervously on stage. Avi turned to Eli.

"Come on, Eli," he whispered. "You were in charge of our class choir this past winter *and*

The Burksfield Bike Club

you have the best voice around. You start a song and we'll sing along."

Eli looked nervously at the crowd of people sitting before the stage. He shrugged his shoulders, closed his eyes and began to sing. The boys automatically followed his lead and sang along.

"MAOZ TZUR YE-SHU-A-SY ..."

Oh, no! thought Avi to himself in embarrassment. *What a song to choose for summertime! It's too late to stop now, though. I guess we'll have to keep singing.*

"LECHAH NA-EH LISHA-BAY-ACH ..."

"VOT'S DOT?" came loudly from the lady in the front row. "OY VEY," she cried. *"They think it's Chanukah time in the summer!"*

"TIKON BAIS TEFILASI ..."

Avi turned to look at his friends. Their cheeks were just as red as his felt.

"Sing *Dreidel, Dreidel*," called out an old man from the back of the room. This was followed by much chuckling and laughter from the pleased audience.

This is really embarrassing, thought Avi to himself.

Avi nudged Eli with his foot to get his attention. He motioned with his hands to end the song after the first stanza.

"AZ EGMOR BESHIR MIZMOR CHANUKAS HAMIZ ... BAY ... ACH."

Mitzvos on Wheels

The Burksfield Bike Club

With that, the members of the Burksfield Bike Club stopped their singing.

There were a few long seconds of silence before one man sitting in a wheelchair clapped softly, to be polite.

Avi whispered to Eli, "Why did you pick a Chanukah song?"

"Well," blushed Eli, "that was the song we sang in our class choir during the winter."

Avi slapped his forehead in despair. "This time pick a song that we sing in the summer," he begged. "Okay?"

"If you say so," said Eli, shrugging his shoulders. "I'll pick my favorite song."

Eli cleared his throat, opened his mouth and once again the beautiful sound of his voice filled the room.

As before, his friends automatically began to sing along. It took about ten seconds for Avi to realize what they were singing.

"TZUR MI-SHELO ... MI-SHELO ACHALNU ..."

Once again, Avi slapped his forehead, and his face turned even redder than before.

"TZUR MI-SHELO ... MI-SHELO ACHALNU ..."

A familiar voice rang out from the front row. "OY VEY!" cried the same old lady. "Foist they think it's Chanukah, now it's Shabbos. Vot kind of mixed up boychiks did they bring us?"

From the corner of his eye Avi noticed a door

Mitzvos on Wheels

on the side of the stage open up. Out popped the head of his Tanta Hadassah. She looked quite surprised to see her nephew and his friends on stage singing Shabbos songs.

"RACHAIM B'CHASDECHA ..."

For a moment she stood there in shock, her hands on her face. Very quickly, she regained her composure and started motioning to Avi.

Avi nodded his head and began nudging and motioning to the boys all around him.

"TZUR MI-SHELO ACHALNU ..."

The boys quickly lined up single file behind Avi and began marching towards the side door. As they marched, they continued singing.

"SAVANU VEHOSARNU KIDVAR ..."

As the final words left their mouths, the boys made a small bow toward the audience and quickly exited.

"Whew!" said Avromy falling against a nearby wall. "I'm sure glad that's over."

"Did that really happen?"

"I've never been so embarrassed in my life!"

"This Shabbos I'm keeping my mouth shut! I've had enough for one week!"

The boys opened the door a crack to see what was happening on the stage they had just left—and burst into loud laughter.

There on stage was Tanta Hadassah, shaking a bright pink tambourine. Following in line

The Burksfield Bike Club

behind her was a group of ten adorable four-year-old girls. Each one wore a pink pocketbook on one arm, a tambourine in the other, and a big cardboard smiley face on her forehead.

Tanta Hadassah introduced them as the Camp Bais Yaakov kindergarten. They began to shake their tambourines and sing a song about being happy.

"I think we sounded *much* better than them!" Eli said, choking with laughter. "Okay Eli," snickered Moish, "we'll get permission for you to sing here again. You can even bring a tambourine!"

Eli, Moish and all the boys laughed so hard they thought they would burst. When there was a pause in the performance Tanta Hadassah came out to meet them.

"Avi," she cried, "what in the world are you doing here? Why were you on that stage singing Shabbos songs?"

Avi smiled. "The part about the singing is a long story, but I'm really here for a very important reason. Do you have a few minutes to meet with us?"

Tanta Hadassah looked at the boys with Avi.

"Are these all the members of the famous Burksfield Bike Club Can Collectors?"

"You mean Burksfield Bike Club—Mitzvos on Wheels," corrected Avi. "Yes, they are. We have something really important to talk to you about."

Mitzvos on Wheels

"Okay," she answered. "Wait here for five more minutes until the girls finish singing. Then I'll talk to you."

Tanta Hadassah quickly ran back to the girl's performance. The boys went out to the main lobby. Some lounged on the easy chairs, others went to the windows overlooking a pretty garden. None of the boys had ever really been to a home for seniors before and were glad to see something besides the stage.

"Look over here!" pointed Avromy.

The boys joined him at a bulletin board hanging in the hallway. Avromy was reading it with great interest.

"This is amazing!" he said.

"What is that?" asked Yitzy.

"There's a picture of each person who lives here," explained Avromy. "Under each picture they wrote a paragraph about their lives."

"Wow!" said Moish. "Look at this one!"

"Mrs. Bertha Feldman," read Eli. "Born in Minsk, Russia. 'I came to America in 1932 at the age of twelve. I have three children and twelve grandchildren. I worked as a manager in Bloom's Department store for forty-seven years. Now I live in Anshei Shalom. The people here are nice, but I miss being busy.'"

"For forty-seven years! Wow, that's a long time. And Bloom's is a very big department store," said

The Burksfield Bike Club

Eli. "I can't imagine such an old lady running that kind of store."

"She wasn't always this old," Moish pointed out.

"Oh, that's true," agreed Eli.

"Look at this one," Avi read. "Hyman Feingold. 'I was born in Burksfield. When I turned fifteen I left my family to travel the world. I spent many years in France, England and Israel. I have recently returned to spend my remaining years in my old hometown.'"

"Hey," Avromy thought out loud, "I wonder if he's related to the Mr. Feingold we know."

Their conversation was interrupted by Tanta Hadassah, minus the tambourine and the four-year-old girls. "Boys," called Tanta Hadassah, "come with me."

The boys quickly fell in line behind Avi's aunt.

"Boy," whispered Avromy to Avi, "your aunt really moves fast."

"All the time," Avi whispered back proudly. "My aunt always wears sneakers because she's always running around doing one mitzvah or another."

Tanta Hadassah led them into a room. Above the doorway hung a sign that read "CONFERENCE ROOM." Inside was a large, wide wooden table with many chairs around it. The chairs were made of black leather and

Mitzvos on Wheels

swiveled. The room had deep, beige carpeting and matching curtains on the big picture window. The boys grinned at one another as they sat down, swiveling even before they landed in the seats. This was certainly a far cry from their usual conference area in the back of Avi's garage!

"Have a seat, everyone," said Tanta Hadassah in a business-like way; she motioned towards the chairs. "What can I do for you?"

All heads turned towards Avi. Avi cleared his throat.

"Well," he began, "we are having a problem with our can collection, and we couldn't think of a solution until suddenly I remembered some wise words that an aunt of mine once told me."

Avi smiled at his aunt and she rewarded him with one of her own.

"And what did this wise aunt tell you?" asked Tanta Hadassah with a wink.

"Well," said Avi, "she told me that *mitzvah goreres mitzvah*, one mitzvah leads to another."

"Those truly are wise words, but what do they have to do with your problem?"

Avi began telling Tanta Hadassah about all the work it would take to clean and sort the cans they were collecting.

"Hmm, that does sound like a lot of work."

The Burksfield Bike Club

"That's right, and if we do all that we won't have any time left to collect new cans."

"I see," said Tanta Hadassah. "What does this have to do with me?"

"Well," Avi went on, "you did tell me that you were looking for something for the people in Shaarei Shalom to do."

Tanta Hadassah's eyes lit up in surprise and understanding.

"Do you mean to say that you want the people in this home to clean and sort the cans for you?"

"Exactly!" said Avi. That special look was still twinkling in his eyes and his eyebrows were only starting to straighten out.

"It would give them something really useful to do," added Moish.

"It's a big mitzvah, too!" added Avromy.

"It's a double mitzvah," Avi finished for them. "Like you said Tanta, '*Mitzvah goreres mitzvah.*'"

Tanta Hadassah rested her chin in her hand and looked thoughtful.

"Hmmm," she said. "I think I like this idea. And I know just the person to put in charge of this project."

"Mrs. Bertha Feldman?" asked Avi with a sly grin.

Tanta Hadassah looked at him in shock.

"How did you know that?"

"A little bulletin board told me," answered Avi

with a smile. "If she can manage a department store she can certainly manage some old cans."

"You really are something, little nephew," she patted Avi on the head affectionately. "I'll have to get permission from the board of directors of this home."

"Do you think they'll agree?" asked Eli.

"I hope so," answered Tanta Hadassah. "I'll call Avi tonight with their answer."

With that their conference ended and the boys all turned to leave.

"Goodbye, Tanta Hadassah," called Avi.

"Goodbye, Mrs. Goodside. Thanks!" echoed his friends.

"Uh oh!" Moish glanced at his watch as they were mounting their bikes. "It's really late. We'd better ride fast if we want to make Mincha."

"Oh no!" cried Avromy as he ran to his bike. "More exercise. That's all I need!"

That night Avi found himself pacing back and forth in front of the phone.

"You look pretty nervous, Avi," said his father. "It must hard to sit here waiting for Tanta Hadassah to call."

"It sure is," answered Avi. "If the people in Shaarei Shalom can't sort the cans for us I don't know how we'll get the job done. And how will we make any money for the yeshiva?"

"Well," said Rabbi Drimler, "let me tell you some happy news to take your mind off of your worries."

"What?" asked Avi with interest. "What's the good news?"

Mitzvos on Wheels

"Do you remember our friends the Berkowitzes?"

"Yes," said Avi. "Blacky's owners."

"That's right," said Rabbi Drimler. "Well, it seems that Mr. and Mrs. Berkowitz will be joining us for Shabbos this week."

"Wow!" shouted Avi, pumping the air with his fist. "That's great!"

"Blacky won't be coming with them though. He'll be staying with a neighbor."

"I'm happy to hear that, too," said Avi with a chuckle.

Just then the phone rang. Avi looked nervously at his father.

"Nu," said Rabbi Drimler gently. "Answer it. Let's see what Hashem has in store for the Burksfield Bike Club."

Avi picked up the phone.

"Hello?" he said nervously.

"Avi," said Tanta Hadassah's voice excitedly. "Good news!"

"What?" asked Avi.

"The board members of Shaarei Shalom like your plan very much. "

"*Yay!*" yelled Avi.

"And," continued Tanta Hadassah, "they want you to start tomorrow."

"Tomorrow? That'll be great!"

"What time will you be delivering the cans?"

The Burksfield Bike Club

The smile slid off of Avi's face like a potato latke off a plate. "Delivering ... the cans?" he asked.

"Of course," said Tanta Hadassah. "You don't expect the people from Shaarei Shalom to come pick them up, do you?"

"Uh ... no, I guess not," said Avi scratching his head. "I just never thought about *how* we would get the cans to you."

"Well," said Tanta Hadassah, "you think about it and let me know."

"Yeah. Okay," mumbled Avi.

"Don't worry, Avi. I'm sure you'll think of something."

Avi felt a little better. "Thank you, Tanta Hadassah. I'll call you when we've got it figured out. Goodbye."

"Good news or bad news?" asked Rabbi Drimler. "I can't tell by your face."

"It's really both," Avi replied. "Shaarei Shalom agreed to take care of the cans, but we need to find a way to bring the cans to Shaarei Shalom."

"Hmm," Rabbi Drimler frowned, "that does seem to be a problem. Well, let's think about it tonight. I'm sure Hashem will send an answer soon."

"I sure hope so, Abba. I really do. Good night."

"Good night, Avi."

Avi said Shema and lay down in bed. How *would* *they* move those cans? Could they possibly schlep

Mitzvos on Wheels

them all the way to Shaarei Shalom by bike, bag by bag? That just seemed too hard.

His parent's car wasn't really big enough. What he really needed was a van or a truck. Suddenly Avi sat up in bed.

"Of course!" he said out loud. "Tzvi Abayakov has a van from his store! I'm sure he will help us out."

After day camp the next day Avi and his friends rode right over to Tzvi's hardware store. They parked their bikes outside and filed in. As they pushed open the door a little bell rang announcing their arrival.

Avi had always loved hardware stores. There were just *so many* interesting things on every shelf. Tzvi's store was wide and well lit. The shelving went way up to the ceiling and every shelf was chock full of gadgets. Packages of nails, screws, hooks and washers were stacked neatly on one side. A whole section of paint, brushes, drop cloths and turpentine were set up in the back. Eli, as if pulled by a magnet, had already wandered off to the section that stocked electrical tape, wiring, switches and packages of cordless phones. The big tools, looking important and professional, were displayed in a glass showcase on the side. Avi had to force his eyes to focus on Tzvi instead of on all the tools around him.

The boys told Tzvi their problem. They were

The Burksfield Bike Club

positive he would volunteer to help them immediately. But to their surprise Tzvi lowered his head regretfully.

"I'm sorry, boys," he said, looking sad. "You know I would love to help you, but I'm sorry to say that my van's engine died yesterday."

"It died?" asked Eli in wonder.

"Well," said Tzvi, "let's just say it stopped working. I don't know when or if I'll be able to afford a new one for a while. Business has been a bit slow lately."

The boys all felt very sorry for their friend Tzvi. They also felt sorry for themselves.

"Listen," said Tzvi, "if there is anything *else* I can do, please let me know. I really feel bad about the cans."

"It's okay, Tzvi. We'll figure something out."

A group of very sad members of the Burksfield Bike Club slowly pedaled back to shul. They went down to the basement and sat down in a circle on the floor. It was time for another conference. The boys looked at each other glumly. Avi noticed Moish staring at him.

"Why are you looking at me like that?" he asked.

"I'm waiting, of course," answered Moish confidently.

"Waiting for what?" asked Avi, a little bit annoyed.

Mitzvos on Wheels

"I'm waiting for you to get that look in your eyes. You know, when your eyes crinkle up, when you have a plan."

"But I don't have any plan!" cried Avi in disappointment.

"You don't?"

"No, I don't."

"But you always have a plan!" Eli said a little desperately.

"Not this time," answered Avi.

"Not even a little one?" asked Eli in a wheedling tone.

"No," answered Avi, growing more annoyed by the minute. "Why don't *you* guys think of a plan?"

After a few silent, thoughtful moments, Avromy's eyes lit up. He whispered something into Moish's ear. Moish smiled and whispered into Eli's ear.

"What? What's going on?" asked Avi, jumping up.

"No, you were right, Avi," smiled Moish. "You always surprise us with your plans. This time let us surprise you with one of ours."

"You mean you know how to get the cans to Shaarei Shalom?"

"Yes," Avromy said looking around to see if his friends agreed. "But we want to surprise you. You go upstairs and call Tanta Hadassah

The Burksfield Bike Club

on the shul's phone. Tell her to get ready for a big delivery. Then wait here. We'll be back for the cans in half an hour."

Before Avi could think of anything to say, Avromy, Moish and Eli quickly got up and headed for the door.

"Wait," Avi called after them, "what will I tell my aunt?"

"Just tell her that we'll be there with the cans at about 3:30!"

"How?" shouted Avi to his friends as he chased after them.

"We said it would be a surprise!" Moish called back. "Just wait here for us!"

Avi went upstairs feeling a little confused. It was usually him at the front of the crowd calling back instructions! What were his friends up to? He went into the office to call his aunt. She was very happy to hear the good news.

Avi returned to the basement.

"Where in the world are they?" he thought to himself looking at the clock. "Oh well, I might as well start piling up the bags neatly."

After a while Avi forgot the time. He worked at getting the cans into some kind of order. Sweating and pulling he piled the bags of cans into a row. Some of the bags were not as strong as others and came apart. A lot of the cans were loose to begin with. He started to feel like some of the

Mitzvos on Wheels

cans actually ran away from him and refused to get into their bags and piles! He was grateful to be interrupted by some loud banging at the door. He quickly jumped to open it and almost fainted at what he saw.

Outside the shul's side door stood a huge crowd of kids. Every kid came with some kind of transportation! There were bikes of all sizes and shapes—mountain bikes, racing bikes, bikes with training wheels and tricycles. Some kids rode skateboards; there were lots of scooters and some were wearing rollerblades. There was even one kid with a jogging stroller! It seemed like every single boy in Burksfield was standing outside the shul ready to roll!

Tzvi Abayakov was walking among them, handing out bags and shopping baskets.

"Ta-daaah!" yelled Avromy and Moish bowing and waving. "What do you think of our plan?"

Avi stood there in shock.

"There must be a hundred people out here!" he said in wonder. "Did you get every boy in town to come?"

"Actually, there's a hundred and nineteen, to be exact," said Moish. His face glowed with pride.

"And not just boys," Eli pointed out. "Look over there."

Avi turned around and heard a loud, familiar "Woof!" He couldn't believe it! There standing

The Burksfield Bike Club

against a fence was Mrs. Berkowitz—with Blacky! Attached to Blacky was a little wooden wagon. Mrs. Berkowitz waved at Avi cheerily.

"Hi, Avi," she called. "When Blacky saw all these boys racing here she wanted to help out, too!"

Avi just smiled—he couldn't think of anything else to do or say.

"Okay, everybody," yelled Moish. "Line up in front of the door with your bags. We'll fill them up for you."

"And when you're finished," added Avromy, "line up by the gate. We'll all ride to Shaarei Shalom together."

A line formed. One at a time all the boys stepped up to the door of the shul's basement. Eli would scoop up a bunch of cans and hand them to Avromy. Avromy would pass them to Moish. Moish would pass them to Avi, and Avi would put them into the bag the boy was holding.

Within an amazingly short time the basement floor was totally emptied of cans.

"Okay, everybody," Avi yelled to the crowd. "Let's get ready to go to Shaarei Shalom."

Everyone lined up. It was an amazing sight—row after row of boys in all sorts of vehicles (and one dog), and each was holding a bag of cans!

Suddenly the sound of a siren pierced the

Mitzvos on Wheels

air. Everyone turned to see where it was coming from.

Seconds later a police car zoomed into sight. It quickly turned into the lot next to the shul and screeched to a stop.

Blacky started barking furiously. Avi almost stopped breathing. What was going on? What had they done wrong?

Nobody said a word. Some of the younger boys began to cry.

The police car door opened and out stepped a familiar sight. It was Officer Jackson.

Everyone breathed a little easier. Every boy in town knew Officer Jackson. He was the officer in charge of dealing with Burksfield's Jewish community. Whenever there was a major Jewish event in town, Officer Jackson was involved. He would make arrangements for traffic control, parking spaces and anything needed for the safety of the Jews of Burksfield.

Although he wasn't Jewish, Officer Jackson was known and loved by the entire Jewish community. The leaders of the community trusted him to do his job and he had become a friend. Sometimes he was even invited to *kiddushim* that people would make on Shabbos. Officer Jackson really loved *kishke*!

Today, however, Officer Jackson did not look as happy as he usually did. In fact, he looked very, very upset.

The Burksfield Bike Club

He looked over the sea of young faces searching for an adult. Finally he spotted Tzvi.

"What's going on here?" he asked loudly. "I got reports of some kind of rally going on at the synagogue. Rabbi Goldenberg never called me about a rally. I have to know about these things, you know."

Tzvi approached the police officer and calmly explained to him what was going on. Avi couldn't hear what Tzvi was saying. He watched nervously as Tzvi pointed to him a few times.

Officer Jackson's face broke out in a smile. He turned to Avi and his friends and addressed them in his booming voice. "You mean you arranged all this on your own, Avi?"

"Well, yes, " Avi spoke for them all. "We knew that Rabbi Goldenberg needed some money so he could build a new Jewish school here."

Officer Jackson put out his hand to give Avi a grown up handshake.

"I know your Rabbi," he said. "He's a very holy man. I think it's wonderful that you children want to go through all this work for him."

Avi breathed a sigh of relief. He shook Officer Jackson's hand confidently.

"But," continued the officer, "it would be very dangerous for so many children to be riding through the streets at one time."

Avi held his breath again.

Mitzvos on Wheels

"Let me see what I can do," he said as he climbed back into his patrol car.

Everyone watched through the police car window as the officer had a conversation over his police radio. After a few very tense moments more sirens were heard. More police cars began pulling up to the shul! Officer Jackson spoke with the other policemen, pointing and gesturing at the boys.

Would they be allowed to go? What would happen if the police made them put the cans back into the shul? The crowd of boys murmured among themselves, worrying. They waited in suspense.

After a few minutes three of the police cars drove off and two remained. Officer Jackson pulled a megaphone out of his car's trunk. He aimed it at the crowd of boys and began to speak.

"Listen up, everyone. Since you are all doing a good deed, we of the Burksfield Police Force are going to lend a hand."

Avi, Eli, Avromy and Moish looked at each other in amazement. The crowd cheered.

"You will be receiving an official police escort. Three squad cars have gone to stop traffic up ahead. My car will be driving in front of you and that other car will ride behind you. Now ride carefully, everyone."

The Burksfield Bike Club

The boys erupted in cheers. They jumped, danced and high-fived one another. They were ready to go! They would succeed after all! Everyone got ready to mount whatever he was riding. Bike helmets were strapped on and sneaker laces retied.

"Thank you, Officer Jackson!" rang out one hundred and nineteen voices.

"You're very welcome," answered the officer over his megaphone as he jogged towards his car.

At once the lights and sirens of both police cars came alive. Officer Jackson pulled out into the street with one hundred and nineteen boys on bikes (and one dog) behind him. Behind the bikes rode the other police car with his lights flashing.

"Wow!" exclaimed Avi to Moish, " a real police escort. This is so exciting!"

"Look around," cried Moish. "There isn't even one car on the road."

"That's because the other police cars stopped traffic," Avromy reminded him.

Suddenly, the boys heard a loud noise overhead. "ZUT ... ZUT ... ZUT ... ZUT ..." They felt a strong gust of wind from above.

"What's that? What's happening?" Moish yelled over the loud swishing sound.

"Look up," pointed Avi holding on to his yarmulke.

Mitzvos on Wheels

The Burksfield Bike Club

Moish and everyone else looked up to see a helicopter hovering above them. Written on the side of the swaying, grey chopper were four big black letters: WBRK.

"WBRK? That's the radio station," cried Eli. "Guys! We're being reported on by the radio!"

High in the air newsman George Walzan was reporting from the scene.

"It's an amazing sight, ladies and gentlemen. There are at least one hundred boys on their bikes riding down the streets of this usually quiet town. Burksfield police say that this is a fundraiser for Burksfield's oldest synagogue, Anshei Burksfield. The synagogue is reported to be building a Sheeva, a religious school for immigrants."

Three blocks away Larry Rosenberg of the *Burksfield Bugle* was walking down the street. His boss Mr. Tate had really liked the picture he had brought in for last week's front page. Now he needed a picture for the next edition of the *Bugle*.

He aimed his camera at a running squirrel. "Nah," he said to himself, "not exciting enough."

Then he heard police sirens. They were coming closer.

"Sorry, squirrel," he apologized, running down the block. "I hear news being made. Maybe I'll take your picture another time."

Mitzvos on Wheels

Larry opened his cell phone as he ran. "Sarah," he yelled to his wife. "Do you hear all those sirens? This sounds like really *big* news. Not just *bikes* like last time. It sounds like they're just around the corner from me now. Maybe this will be my big chance!"

Sarah was very excited. "What? What is it?"

"I don't believe it!" Larry was breathless.

"What?" screamed Sarah. " I can't see through the phone, you know! Don't keep me in suspense! What is this big news you're taking pictures of?"

"Bikes!" Larry screamed back. "More bikes! Hundreds of kids on bikes! Bikes, skateboards, scooters everywhere!"

"Larry, are you feeling okay?" asked Sarah astounded.

Larry didn't answer. He collapsed on a nearby bench after taking his third picture. And there he sat, watching as the "parade" passed swiftly by.

The boys enjoyed every minute of their exciting ride with the police. It seemed all too soon that they were pulling up to the entrance of Shaarei Shalom.

Officer Jackson pulled over his car, got out and walked over to Avi.

"Listen, son," he said. "Why don't you go inside by yourself and get them ready for your delivery. I don't think they'd appreciate having a hundred kids running around in there."

Avi nodded his agreement and ran towards the building.

Officer Jackson got back on his megaphone and asked everyone to wait quietly.

Mitzvos on Wheels

Avi entered Shaarei Shalom and quickly ran over to the front desk. "Hello," he said to the woman sitting behind it. "I'm here to see Mrs. Hadassah Goodside."

The woman peered down at Avi over her glasses. "Have you brought the cans that she has been speaking so much about?"

"Yes, I have," Avi answered politely.

The woman pointed to a staircase door. "You'll find her downstairs in the basement."

"Thank you very much," said Avi as he ran towards the door and down the steep flight of stairs.

When he reached the bottom of the staircase Avi paused for a moment. He heard a very loud voice booming from the other side of the door. He opened the door a crack and peeked out.

What he saw almost made him laugh out loud.

Twenty-one elderly men and women were standing against a wall. They stood at perfect attention like soldiers in the army, each wearing what looked like a uniform. Each had on a long plastic apron, rubber gloves and some kind of funny hat over their heads.

Pacing back and forth in front of this small army was a short, stout woman who was barking orders to them.

"This is our mission," she told her troops. "It's an important job, and we're going to do it well. *DO YOU UNDERSTAND ME?*" she thundered.

The Burksfield Bike Club

"Yes, Bertha," they all answered obediently.

"So that's Bertha Feldman," Avi thought to himself.

He took a good look at her. She was very old but not much taller than Avi. She wore a long white plastic apron over a bright pink housecoat. Perched on her head was a bright pink and orange shower cap. On her hands were the biggest yellow rubber gloves Avi had ever seen.

"It looks like they're all ready for our delivery," he thought to himself.

Avi gently knocked on the door. It was opened quickly by Tanta Hadassah.

"Come on in, Avi," she said warmly. "Did you bring the cans?"

"Oh yes," he answered with a smile. "We brought every last can."

"Then bring them on in!" shouted Bertha. "We're ready for them!"

"Can someone come up to get the cans?" asked Avi.

"Of course not," answered Tanta Hadassah. "*These are elderly people, Avi,*" she whispered to him.

"How should I get them down here, then?" Avi asked.

"Well," said Tanta Hadassah, "I guess whoever helped you bring them here should help you carry them down."

Mitzvos on Wheels

The Burksfield Bike Club

Avi's eyes grew big. "Are you sure?" he asked looking doubtful.

"I'm positive! Now get going, Avi," she said, shooing him out the door. "You and all your helpers should bring in those cans right away."

"*All* my helpers?" asked Avi.

"Yes! Yes! Yes!" cried Tanta Hadassah. "Just bring down those cans."

"Okay," said Avi shrugging his shoulders. He climbed back up the staircase and exited the building.

"Look," cried Moish. "Avi finally came out."

Avi did not walk over to his friends, though. He walked straight over to Officer Jackson and began whispering in his ear.

At first, Officer Jackson stared at Avi in disbelief. Then he just shrugged his shoulders and handed Avi the megaphone.

"OKAY, EVERYBODY," Avi yelled into the megaphone. "GET OFF YOUR BIKES, GRAB YOUR BAGS OF CANS AND FOLLOW ME INSIDE."

There was a roar from the crowd as everyone did as they were told. Avi happily led the crowd in.

The woman at the front desk came very close to fainting when she saw the one hundred and nineteen boys swarming through the front doors of Shaarei Shalom.

Avi led them over to the staircase door. He opened it, and then quickly shut it. There would

Mitzvos on Wheels

never be enough room for so many boys to get down the staircase at once.

"Everybody stop!" he cried.

The crowd of boys suddenly came to a halt.

"Listen, everybody," he yelled. "We can't all fit down there at one time. Let's make one long line and we'll pass the bags of cans from one person to another until they're all down there."

A murmur of approval rose from the crowd.

Avi stationed himself at the bottom of the staircase. Behind him was Moish, then Avromy, then Eli, then the one hundred and nineteen other boys. Each one passed his bag down the line until it came to Avi. Avi then brought the bags into the basement area where Bertha and her crew were waiting.

Megaphone still in his hand, Officer Jackson squeezed himself down the staircase. He just *had* to see what was going on.

He entered the room and just stood their staring in disbelief. Bertha took notice of the policeman and walked right over to him. She graced him with her biggest smile. She was positively beaming.

"Oh, Officer Jackson," she gushed, "thank you so much for offering us your protection. You members of the Burksfield Police force are always so helpful."

A speechless Officer Jackson just nodded his head.

The Burksfield Bike Club

"And speaking of being helpful," she continued as she reached for his megaphone, "I hope you won't mind if I borrow this *tchachkelah* for just a little bit."

Officer Jackson looked on in shock as the elderly woman grabbed his megaphone and began immediately shouting orders into it.

"Group One," she bellowed. "That's right—Sidney, Hymie and Irving. You three schlep those bags over to the center of the room. Group Two—that's Sadie, Rosie and Florence. You empty the cans into the sink. Group Three—that's Morris, Abe and Joel—you dry them. Next will be Group Four—Gertrude, Sarah and Ray. You sort them into the three bins."

Avi couldn't stop himself from smiling. Bertha Feldman was definitely doing what she did best and enjoying every minute of it.

Avi noticed Avromy whispering to his Tanta Hadassah. He was curious as to what they were talking about. *I'll have to ask Avromy about it later*, he thought to himself.

After watching for a few minutes the boys went back upstairs. All their one hundred and nineteen helpers—and Blacky—were once again gathered outside.

Moish whispered something into Avi's ear. Avi nodded his approval. Then Avi stood up on a tree trunk and began to speak to the crowd.

"Listen everyone," he began. "Thank you all so much for helping out. As you know, the money from these cans will be going to help Rabbi Goldenberg build a new yeshiva for Iranian boys. When you get home please ask your parents to save their empty cans and bottles. Bring them here as soon as you can."

When Avi finished, Officer Jackson began to speak, without a megaphone this time. "And everyone, please ride home safely," he announced. "For your safety we will have extra police officers on the streets for the next half hour. Please proceed home now."

As they watched all the boys ride off on their bikes, Avi heard Officer Jackson mutter something to himself about needing a nice long vacation.

Shabbos was coming and Avi was getting ready in his bedroom, all smiles. What a week it had been! He kept thinking back to last week and the conversation at the Shabbos table about *mitzvah goreres mitzvah*. So many mitzvos had been done this week because of the Burksfield Bike Club. *There really had been many "Mitzvos on Wheels" this week*, he thought to himself.

Now, right downstairs, another mitzvah was happening because of them. Mr. & Mrs. Berkowitz, owners of Blacky the dog, had just come to his home. They were very excited about experiencing their first real Shabbos.

Mitzvos on Wheels

That night the Drimlers spent a lot of time patiently explaining everything they were doing to the Berkowitzes. They were very eager to learn everything they could. It was all so new and exciting for them.

To his surprise Mr. Berkowitz had enjoyed the davening in Anshei Burksfield very much. He had been nervous when he first entered the shul. His hair and clothes were a little bit different than everyone else's and he couldn't read from the siddur, but Rabbi Drimler had helped him follow along with an English edition. He had not expected to be surrounded by the warm group of people eager to shake his hand and wish him a "good Shabbos" after davening. Rabbi Goldenberg's heartfelt greeting had especially impressed Mr. Berkowitz. He left the building that night with a warm, glowing feeling.

At the Shabbos table, the Berkowitzes enjoyed the food, zemiros and divrei Torah. As Mrs. Berkowitz said, it was not like anything they could have imagined.

Just before Bentching, Mr. Berkowitz turned to Avi. "Now, Avi," he said with a smile, "can you please explain what my wife has been talking about all week? She keeps telling me about you, and cans and a 'sheeva.' What in the world is she talking about?"

The Burksfield Bike Club

Avi smiled. "You must mean the 'yeshiva,'" he corrected. "Let me try to explain."

Avi told Mr. Berkowitz all about Rabbi Goldenberg's plans to build the yeshiva and how he and his friends were trying to raise the twenty thousand dollars needed. He described all the adventures that the Burksfield Bike Club had experienced this past week. They all laughed heartily at the story of the boys' involuntary concert and marveled at how all the pieces had fallen into place at the senior citizens home.

"That yeshiva would have really been nice," said Shmulie.

"What do you mean *would* have been nice?" asked Avi. "It *will* be nice. It will be a beautiful yeshiva with lots of Torah learned in it."

"No," said Shmulie. "I heard Tatty and Ima talking on erev Shabbos."

"*Shhhh*, Shmulie ... let's not talk about this now," said Mrs. Drimler nervously.

"What do you mean?" Avi turned to his father. "Tatty," he pleaded, "please tell me what Shmulie is talking about. Did something happen?"

Rabbi Drimler sighed. "I'm sorry, Avi. I wasn't going to tell you about this until after Havdalah. I didn't want to ruin your Shabbos."

"What? What is it?" asked Avi nervously.

"Rabbi Goldenberg called me before Shabbos

Mitzvos on Wheels

and he sounded very sad. It seems that the contractor called him."

"What's a contractor?" interrupted Shmulie.

"A contractor is someone who fixes or builds houses and buildings," answered Rabbi Drimler. "The contractor called because he hadn't spoken to Rabbi Goldenberg in a month."

"And what did the contractor tell Rabbi Goldenberg?" Avi asked.

"He told him that even if the shul did have the twenty thousand dollars, he still wouldn't have enough time to finish the job before September."

Avi's face fell.

"I guess that means that there won't be a new yeshiva this year," said Shmulie.

"Yeah," agreed Avi sadly, "and all our work was for nothing."

The Drimler Shabbos table, which was usually happy and loud, became very silent. No one knew what to say.

"Excuse us for a moment," said Mr. Berkowitz, suddenly breaking the silence. Mr. and Mrs. Berkowitz got up and left the table. Without the guests at the table, Rabbi Drimler spoke plainly and simply to his son.

"My dear Avi," he said, placing a hand on his son's arm affectionately. "I know you worked very hard on this mitzvah project. Your mother and I are extremely proud of what you've done. I also

Mitzvos on Wheels

know that the news we've just heard is very sad. There is one thing we must keep in mind though. Today is Shabbos. We have a mitzvah to be happy on Shabbos no matter what. You don't want our guests to feel bad on their first special Shabbos. So try not to be too unhappy. You'll see that in the end everything will work out for the best."

"You're right, Tatty," mumbled Avi, brushing away a tear. "I feel so bad. I ruined our Shabbos table and made it sad and uncomfortable. It made the Berkowitzes want to walk away."

"That's not why we walked away," called Mrs. Berkowitz from across the room. "We walked away because we thought we knew how to make this Shabbos table happy again."

"You do?" Everyone was surprised and curious.

Mr. Berkowitz turned towards Rabbi Drimler.

"Do you remember the Torah thought you told me in shul? About ... what were those words? ... 'Shkocho Protists'?"

"Yes, you mean *Hashgacha Pratis*," agreed Rabbi Drimler.

"Yes, exactly," answered Mr. Berkowitz. "Shkocho Protist. You said that sometimes we can see clearly how Hashem's hand is guiding everything that's going on."

"That's correct," Rabbi Drimler praised him. "You're a fast learner."

The Burksfield Bike Club

"Well," continued Mr. Berkowitz, "this is definitely one of those times."

"What do you mean?"

"You see," said Mr. Berkowitz, "I just happen to be a contractor myself."

"You are?" cried Avi.

"Yes, I am," Mr. Berkowitz smiled at him. "I also think very highly of your Rabbi, Rabbi Goldenberg. If he wants this 'sheeva' built so badly, then I would be happy to make sure it gets done before September."

"You would?" cried Avi jumping out of his seat.

"I certainly would," answered Mr. Berkowitz, "and I'm not going to charge Rabbi Goldenberg twenty thousand dollars to do the job either."

"You're not?" Avi was hopping with excitement.

"Of course not," answered Mr. Berkowitz. "I refuse to make a profit off of such a holy man, who's doing such holy work."

"That's right," added Mrs. Berkowitz. "My husband will make sure the price is very low, and we will work it out so that Rabbi Goldenberg doesn't have to pay us all the money at once. With the help of Avi's can project, I'm sure he'll be able to pay my husband for everything within a year or so."

"This really is *Hashgacha Pratis*, Mr. Berkowitz, but business is something that should be discussed after Shabbos. For now, let's just end

Mitzvos on Wheels

this conversation with a big 'thank you,'" said Rabbi Drimler with a warm smile.

"Hey, it's the least we can do to help out the Rabbi of our new shul," said Mr. Berkowitz.

"Anshei Burksfield isn't a new shul," piped up Shmulie from under the table. "It's an old one!"

"I said *our* new shul," replied Mr. Berkowitz, smiling at his wife.

A huge grin broke out across Rabbi Drimler's face. "Thank you, Mr. and Mrs. Berkowitz. Thank you and welcome to our community."

"Do you mean ... ?" Avi was almost under the table himself.

"Yes," Mr. Berkowitz finished Avi's thought for him. "My wife and I both agree that it's time for us to live more like Jews should. Part of doing that will mean going to shul regularly."

Mrs. Drimler gave Mrs. Berkowitz a big hug. There were both smiles and tears all around.

"This is really great news," whispered Shmulie to Avi as the adults continued talking quietly.

"No," answered Avi. "It isn't new; it's just like it says in *Pirkei Avos*: 'Mitzvah goreres mitzvah.'"

Bright and early Sunday morning the members of the Burksfield Bike Club found themselves once again in the basement of Anshei Burksfield.

"Boy," said Eli, "this place has gotten so much bigger since we got rid of the cans."

"That's for sure," agreed Moish. "Nu, Avi," he continued, "what's the big news that you wanted to tell us?"

Avi told them what had happened at his Shabbos table on Friday night. They listened intently as he described the details. Everyone was thrilled that Rabbi Goldenberg's dream of a yeshiva was close to coming true. They were

Mitzvos on Wheels

also amazed at how the Berkowitzes lives were changing—all because of their little "mitzvah can project."

"Wow!" cried Eli. "That's great news. It's hard to believe all that's happened."

"Now that the situation has changed, is there anything else that we need to be doing?" asked Avromy.

"Well," said Avi, "I spoke to my aunt this morning before I came here. She told me that the people in Shaarei Shalom are really enjoying taking care of the cans. They are almost finished cleaning and sorting them."

"Boy," said Avromy, "that was a lot of cans. They really work fast."

"What are they going to do with the cans?" asked Moish.

"That's our next job," answered Avi. "We need to call the soda companies and ask them to come pick them up."

"Oh, I'll do that," volunteered Eli. "Mr. Applebaum gave me the numbers of the companies to call. I'll go upstairs and call them right now."

With that Eli ran from the room. On his way out, he almost bumped into Tzvi Abayakov.

"Hi, Tzvi," yelled all the boys.

"Hello, boys," Tzvi greeted them warmly. "I must say, you've done it again. Rabbi Goldenberg is walking around like the happiest man in the world."

The Burksfield Bike Club

"Don't thank us," said Avi. "Thank the Berkowitzes."

"Yes," said Tzvi. "I heard about the amazing *Hashgacha Pratis* of Mr. Berkowitz being a contractor."

"And his wife is a banker!" added Avi.

"Yes, yes," said Tzvi, "truly amazing."

Eli came back into the room looking a little downcast. "Guys," he said, "I have some bad news."

"Oh no," groaned Moish, "what now? I thought we were home free."

"Well," Eli told them, "I spoke to a person in each soda company. They all told me the same thing. They said that unless we are a business that sells their soda they won't pick up the cans from us."

"Uh oh," said Avi, "that's a big problem."

"Maybe not," said Eli. "They said that we can bring them the cans any day of the week, and they will give us the money."

"I wish I had my van," said Tzvi. "I would be more than happy to pick up and deliver those cans."

"Hmm," Avi thought out loud, "who else do we know with a big truck or van?"

After a few moments of thought Tzvi was the one to come up with the solution. "I've got it!" he cried.

Mitzvos on Wheels

"What do you have?" asked Eli.

"I've got a great idea!" cried Tzvi happily. "I know the perfect person to pick up those cans."

"Who is it?" asked the boys all together.

Tzvi smiled. "Okay, boys, now it's my turn! Let me surprise you! Meet me at Shaarei Shalom in twenty minutes."

The four friends found themselves pedaling down that familiar road from shul to Shaarei Shalom.

Eli said what was on everyone's mind: "This trip was a lot more fun last time ..."

"Well," Moish answered sensibly, "we can't have a police escort *every* time we go somewhere!"

When they got to Shaarei Shalom, the boys were happy to find Tanta Hadassah just leaving.

"Boys," she cried, "you wouldn't believe what your cans have done."

"What do you mean?" Avi answered her playfully. "Cans can't do as much as sneakers do."

"You're wrong," answered his aunt. "Your cans made Bertha Feldman smile again. They made Joel Sugarstein stand up a little straighter."

"Our cans did that?" asked Eli.

"That's right," answered Tanta Hadassah. "Until now, many of the people living in Shaarei Shalom felt bored and useless. Now with this can project they feel useful again. They are helping to build a yeshiva. That's an important job and they're proud to do it."

"That's great," said Avi. All the boys nodded their heads in agreement.

"It's too bad that we don't have any more cans to bring them," said Eli.

"What do you mean?" asked Tanta Hadassah. "Since you brought that crowd here last week, boys from the neighborhood have been bringing more and more cans every day."

"*Gevaldik!*" laughed Avromy.

"So what are you boys doing here now?" Tanta Hadassah asked.

"We're waiting for Tzvi to come with a van to take away the cans."

"Oh, okay," Tanta Hadassah told them as she hurried away. "The cans are all neatly organized and waiting at the bottom of the steps. Good luck."

"Thank you," the boys called after her.

They all leaned against the gate as they waited for Tzvi, except for Avromy who ran after Avi's aunt. "Mrs. Goodside," he called. "Can I talk to you for a minute?"

"Sure, Avromy," she said turning to the boy.

Avi couldn't hear what his aunt and friend were talking about, but he was certainly curious as to what it was about.

Mitzvos on Wheels

Avromy returned to his friends with a big smile on his face.

"What's going on?" asked Avi. "That's the second time you've had a secret conversation with my aunt."

"Well," answered Avromy with a shy smile on his face, "it's not really a secret, but I didn't want to say anything until I was sure."

"Sure about what?" asked Eli anxiously.

"I wasn't sure about Hymie," answered Avromy.

"Who's Hymie," cried Avi, "and why do you need to be sure about him?" All the boys surrounded Avromy and stood eagerly waiting for his explanation.

"Let me start from the beginning," he said. "Do you remember the day that we sang here?"

"Remember it?" cried Moish. "I'll never forget it. It was one of the most embarrassing things I've ever done."

"Yes," said Avromy. "Now do you remember what we did right after we sang?

"Sure," said Avi, "we waited in the hallway to speak to my aunt."

"And we were reading the bulletin boards," said Eli. "We read about Bertha Feldman, and Hyman Feingold."

"Exactly!" cried Avromy. "Well, that's what I was speaking to Mrs. Goodside about."

The Burksfield Bike Club

"So ... what about Hyman Feingold?" asked Moish.

"Well," said Avromy, "it said on the bulletin board that Hyman left home at the age of fifteen. It didn't sound like he ever had anything to do with his family again."

"Okay," said Avi, "so what?"

"So," continued Avromy, "I noticed two things about Hyman. Number one, his name sounded familiar. Number two, his picture looked very similar to someone I know."

Avi's eyes grew wide. "You mean that you think he is Max Feingold's long-lost brother?"

Avromy grinned from ear to ear. "That is exactly right!" he cried. "Your aunt did some research for me, and she found out that it's true. Max and Hyman really are long-lost brothers. They both live in Burksfield but each one has no idea he has a brother living a few blocks away."

"WOW!" cried the other three boys at once.

"Your aunt is arranging for the two brothers to meet tomorrow in Shaarei Shalom."

"That's great," cried Avi. "Maybe Tanta Hadassah and Hyman will be able to convince Mr. Feingold to come live in Shaarei Shalom, too, instead of staying home by himself all the time."

Suddenly a loud explosion interrupted their conversation.

Mitzvos on Wheels

"What was that?" yelled Moish spinning around.

They all turned to stare down the block. Their jaws hung open in astonishment at the sight in front of them.

Coming slowly down the block, making a loud *put-put* sound as it crawled along, was a very, very old truck. Sitting in the front seat were two men who appeared to be waving at them.

"What ... who ... in the world is that?" asked Eli.

As the truck drew closer, the boys were able to make out the face of the person in the passenger seat. It was Tzvi Abayakov waving wildly at them. A big smile lit up his face.

"Who's driving that thing?" asked Avi.

The boys all strained their eyes to see.

It was almost impossible to make out the face of the driver because he was so short. All that could be seen over the steering wheel was a bald head, bobbing up and down as the truck bounced along the road.

As the truck drew nearer, the boys were able to make out the picture of a large seltzer bottle on its side. Over the picture were large letters.

"SELTZER'S SELTZER," Avi read out loud.

The boys all turned to each other, eyes wide with wonder.

"Nah!" said Avi. "It couldn't be!"

The Burksfield Bike Club

Suddenly there was another explosion. The boys turned back to the truck to see a cloud of black smoke spewing from its tailpipe. There was so much smoke that they couldn't even see the truck anymore. Everyone began to cough and choke.

"Hello boyehs!" cried a familiar voice from inside the smoke. "How do you like mein truck?"

Avi looked up, and sure enough there sitting behind the wheel was none other than Mr. Seltzer from Anshei Burksfield.

"You sell seltzer?" Avi asked with a wheeze.

"Vat then?" exclaimed Mr. Seltzer with a smile. "With a name like Seltzer you thought maybe I sold pickles?"

Everyone burst out laughing.

"I retired seven years ago," continued Mr. Seltzer, "but I still have mein truck. I keep her in mein garage."

"Nu," said Tzvi, "let's get to work already. Mr. Seltzer and I will open up the back of the truck; you boys go get the cans."

The boys ran quickly into Shaarei Shalom. After a number of trips up and down the stairs, all of the cans were safely inside Mr. Seltzer's truck.

"Come on boyehs!" cried Mr. Seltzer. "Put your bikes in the beck too. You ken come along for the ride."

Mitzvos on Wheels

The Burksfield Bike Club

"Do you think we should be doing this?" asked Moish with concern as he lifted his bike onto the truck.

"Why not?" asked Avi as he jumped up into the back.

"I'm not so sure about how safe this truck is," answered Moish.

"Don't vurry," cried Mr. Seltzer, "mein truck is safe. She's just a little old—like me."

"BOOM!" went the truck again, causing Moish to jump two feet into the air.

"Don't mind the noyes," joked Mr. Seltzer. "Mein truck just has a little bit of heartboin, like me after the kigel in sheel."

As the ancient truck rumbled down the street, the boys held on tight.

They drove to three different soda companies. At each stop, Tzvi and the boys got out to schlep the cans inside and collect the deposit money. After all the deposit money had been collected their grand total was four hundred and seventeen dollars.

"That's a pretty nice amount of money," commented Avromy. He was pleased and proud.

"And people are bringing in more and more cans every day," added Avi.

"I vood take the kens in for you every week," offered Mr. Seltzer. "Mein truck and I are heppy to do mitzvois."

Mitzvos on Wheels

Unexpectedly, there was a loud *"RING RING"* sound in the truck.

"What's that?" asked Avromy.

"Oh, that's my cell phone," answered Tzvi, reaching into his pocket. "Excuse me for a minute."

Tzvi put the cell phone to his ear. "Hello," he said. "Oh, hello Rabbi Goldenberg. How are you?"

They watched as Tzvi's eyes suddenly bulged out.

"What did you say? FIVE HUNDRED DOLLARS? I don't believe it!"

"What? What? What?" whispered Avi, Moish, Avromy and Eli all at once.

Tzvi motioned to them to wait another minute and continued speaking into the phone.

"Yes," he said. "Avi and his friends are with me right now. I'll tell them right away. Goodbye."

The boys could hardly keep themselves standing as they hung over the front seat to hear what Tzvi had to say.

"Tell us, Tzvi," they all cried together, "what did Rabbi Goldenberg say?"

"You're not going to believe this, boys," he replied, "but Rabbi Goldenberg said he received forty checks in the mail! It seems that many people heard about your bicycle trip to Shaarei

The Burksfield Bike Club

Shalom last week on the radio. They all wanted to help. All together, the checks added up to five hundred dollars."

"Wow!" cried the four boys at once, slapping each other and hooting with joy.

"And," continued Tzvi, "I imagine that there will be even more checks coming in for at least the next few days."

"That's unbelievable!" said Eli.

"That's fantastic!" cried Moish.

"That's ... *mitzvah goreres mitzvah!*" shouted Avi.

"BOOM!" agreed Mr. Seltzer's ancient truck as it rattled and banged its way back to Anshei Burksfield.

Six weeks later the boys found themselves sitting at the *Chanukas Habayis* of the brand new "Yeshiva Bais HaTorah."

Rabbi Goldenberg had never looked happier. His face was glowing with pride and happiness. The entire town of Burksfield had come out for the great occasion. Roshei Yeshiva from all over the country had also come to give their blessings to the new yeshiva.

The Burksfield Bike Club boys sat in their stiff white Shabbos shirts looking around at the huge crowd. They were a little embarrassed because Rabbi Goldenberg had given them special seats of honor, all the way in the front

The Burksfield Bike Club

row. They were even more embarrassed when he mentioned them by name in his speech. Rabbi Goldenberg was a special man and knew just how to arrange his words. His praises were gentle, just like when he had kissed them on the head in the shul basement.

It seemed like it had all happened ages ago. Avi was filled with happiness as he gazed at the large crowd. He smiled as he looked at Max and Hyman Feingold sitting next to each other and talking excitedly like young boys.

Behind them sat Mr. and Mrs. Berkowitz, with Blacky at their feet. They were having a spirited conversation with one of the visiting Roshei Yeshiva.

Nearby sat Bertha Feldman and all her helpers from Shaarei Shalom. They were talking and giggling like happy schoolchildren. This was quite an event for them.

So many people, thought Avi, *and so many mitzvos!*

Moish turned to him. "You know, Avi," he said, "some of your plans really are pretty good, after all."

Avi smiled back and looked off into the distance.

"Oh no!" cried Moish.

"What's the matter?" Avromy and Eli turned to them.

Mitzvos on Wheels

The Burksfield Bike Club

"Look at Avi." Moish didn't know whether to laugh or cry. "He's got that look in his eye again!"

Everyone turned to stare at Avi.

Avi didn't say a word. He simply grinned from ear to ear.

Glossary

All terms are Hebrew unless indicated as Yiddish (Yid.) or Aramaic (Aram.).

Bais Medrash—house of Torah study
Bentching (Yidd.)—reciting Grace after Meals
Bikur cholim—attending to the needs of the sick
Bli neder—without promising
Boychiks (Yidd.)—little boys
Bracha—a blessing
Chanukas Habayis—inauguration of a new building
Chavrusa (Aram.)—learning partner
Chazal—acronym for "Chachomeinu, zichronam livracha," our Sages, may their memory be for a blessing
Chessed—kindness
Chillul Hashem—desecration of G-d's name
Divrei Torah—words of Torah
Eretz Yisroel—the land of Israel
Erev Shabbos—Friday, before Shabbos
Gabbai—synagogue attendant
Gemara (Aram.)—Talmud
Gevaldik (Yidd.)—great
Hashgacha Pratis—Divine providence
Havdalah—blessing recited over wine at the conclusion of Shabbos
Hishtadlus—effort
Kiddush— blessing recited over wine at the beginning of Shabbos
Kiddush Hashem—sanctification of G-d's name

The Burksfield Bike Club

Kishke (Yidd.)—stuffed derma, a traditional Shabbos food
Lekavod Shabbos—for the honor of Shabbos
Mah Nishtana—the Four Questions that the youngest child present asks at the seder on the first night of Passover
Mincha—the afternoon prayer
Mishnah—the oral Torah law as codified by R' Yehudah HaNassi
Mitzvah—a Torah-based commandment
Nachas—pride
Negel vasser (Yidd.)—washing one's hands upon awaking in the morning
Neshama—soul
Pasuk—verse from the Torah
Pirkei Avos—Ethics of the Fathers
Pushkas (Yidd.)—charity boxes
Rebbeim—Torah teachers
Roshei Yeshiva—heads of Torah schools
Rugalach (Yidd.)—traditional rolled pastries
Seforim—holy books
Shaitel—wig
Shehakol—blessing recited over foods to which other, more specific blessings do not apply
Shema—the prayer recited each morning and night, affirming G-d's singular existence and accepting the yoke of Divine sovereignty
Shul (Yidd.)—synagogue
Siddur—prayer book
Tchachkelah (Yidd.)—trinket
Tefillah, tefillos—prayer(s)
Tehillim—Psalms
Tisha B'av—the ninth of Av, on which both the first and second Temple were destroyed
Tzedakah—charity
Tzitzis—fringes worn on four-cornered garments by Jewish men and boys
Yeshiva Ketana—Jewish elementary school
Yetzer Hara—the evil inclination
Yetzias Mitzrayim—the Exodus from Egypt
Yidden (Yidd.)—Jews
Yiddishkeit (Yidd.)—Judaism
Yom Tov—a Jewish holiday
Zemiros—special songs for Shabbos or Yom Tov